Hayfoot, Strawfoot

Bucktail Monument
Driftwood, Pennsylvania

Hayfoot, Strawfoot

The Bucktail Recruits

May 4, 2019
To KENNY JOHNS
William P. Robertson

by
William P. Robertson
and
David Rimer

WHITE MANE KIDS
SHIPPENSBURG, PENNSYLVANIA

For a complete list of available publications
please write
White Mane Kids
Division of White Mane Publishing Company, Inc.
P.O. Box 708
Shippensburg, PA 17257-0708 USA
Our Catalog is also available online www.whitemane.com

Library of Congress Cataloging-in-Publication Data

Robertson, William P.
      Hayfoot, Strawfoot : the Bucktail recruits / by William P. Robertson and David Rimer.
         p. cm. -- (White mane kids)
      Includes bibliographical references (p.).
      Summary: Two innocent boys from a backwater hamlet march off to the turmoil of the
   Civil War and bond to face the rigors of army life and the hope for glory,
      ISBN 1-57249-250-3
      1. Kane, Thomas Leiper, 1822-1883 2. United States. Army. Pennsylvania Infantry
   Regiment, 42nd (1861-1864) [1. United States--History--Civil War, 1861-1865--Fiction.]
   I. Rimer, David. II. Title. III. WM kids.

PZ7.R54913 Hay 2001
[Fic]--dc21

                                                                                    2001046578

PRINTED IN THE UNITED STATES OF AMERICA

Contents

Acknowledgments

This book would not have been possible without the help of the Cameron County Historical Society, the McKean County Historical Society, the Warren County Historical Society, and the Reference Department of the Warren Library Association. A special thanks goes to local historians PAUL W. ROBERTSON, RICHARD ROBERTSON, PAUL GELESKIE, SANDRA HORNUNG, and RHONDA J. HOOVER. Thanks also to BROTHER ESKLUND, missionary curator of the Kane Family Museum located at the Church of Jesus Christ of Latter Day Saints in Kane, Pennsylvania. Finally, we would like to applaud WADE ROBERTSON, ELIZABETH KLUNGNESS, MARCIA RIMER, SUE CARLETTA, MARIANNE ZINN, and JILL GIAMANCO for their helpful suggestions. All photos were taken by WILLIAM P. ROBERTSON.

Introduction

The Bucktails were one of the most celebrated Union regiments of the War Between the States. Sworn into service on June 12, 1861, this unit was officially named the 13th Pennsylvania Reserves. It also was known as the First Pennsylvania Rifles, the Kane Rifles, and the 42nd Pennsylvania Volunteers. No matter what name it went by, the regiment's rugged woodsmen gained a reputation for their marksmanship and valor. From Dranesville to Antietam to Gettysburg to the Wilderness, the Bucktails fought with a tenacity that rose to legendary proportions.

Colonel Thomas L. Kane began recruiting men for this new regiment in April of 1861 after gaining permission from Governor Andrew G. Curtin. Kane, the first Pennsylvanian to answer President Abraham Lincoln's call for 70,000 volunteers, chose the McKean County seat of Smethport as his original headquarters. There he enlisted a company of one hundred hardy hunters and lumberjacks. It is the purpose of this novel to trace the adventures of the McKean County Company on its way to Harrisburg across the vast wilderness of northwestern Pennsylvania and into battle in northern Virginia.

These events are presented from the perspective of two fictional recruits. Although this account is based on historical fact, the exploits of the enlisted men and officers, other than Colonel Kane's, were gleaned from local folklore. The novel's title evolved from a training method officers used to teach raw recruits to march in cadence. If a man didn't know his left foot from his right, hay was tied to his left boot and straw to the right. Even the dullest backwoods volunteer knew hay from straw and would soon learn rudimentary marching drills. Of course, the "Bucktail" was a reference to the deer tail or hide the riflemen attached to their kepi caps to identify them as accomplished woodsmen.

General Thomas L. Kane Monument
Kane, Pennsylvania

The Bucktails' Route to War

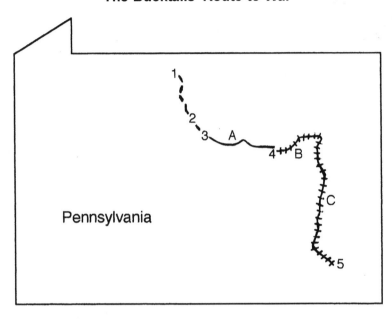

Pennsylvania

Key

1. **Smethport**—Thomas Kane musters in the McKean County Company of Bucktails
2. **Emporium**—Kane's Bucktails arrive here after a grueling march through the Allegheny wilderness
3. **Driftwood**—After being joined by the Cameron County and Elk County Companies, Kane orders rafts built for a white water ride down the Sinnemahoning River
4. **Lock Haven**—The Bucktails take railroad to Harrisburg
5. **Harrisburg**—The Bucktails receive basic training at Camp Curtin, located near the city
A. **Sinnemahoning River**
B. **Philadelphia & Erie Railroad**
C. **Northern Central Railroad**

Chapter One

HARD LESSONS

The ferns rustled, and a lean shadow of a man clad in worn buckskins slid into the glen. His face was hawklike, intense. A scalp lock bristled like quills atop his head. Cradled in his arm was a Kentucky rifle that was as much a part of him as the hand that held it. He sniffed the air like a beast, alert to every scent, sound, and movement.

The ferns rustled again to reveal a second, smaller hunter. The boy had a loose gait to his walk, and a watchfulness pivoted his dark eyes. Like his father he wore buckskins and was armed with a long rifle. He, too, knew every path and grove and thicket of the forested hollow the hunters called home.

Iroquois gestured to his son, Bucky, with hand signals that would go undetected by the creatures they stalked. A glance, a few motions were all they needed to communicate. They had hunted together often.

Falling leaves made more noise than did the hunters slinking through the open woods. They came to a laurel-infested jumble of rocks that cut their visibility to a few feet in any direction. Here they inched along, cautiously peering through the leathery-leaved shrubs that grew higher than a man's head. Bucky edged closer to his father as the shadows grew deeper near a towering block of granite.

Suddenly, the lean man stopped and motioned toward a patch of blueberries that grew between two clumps of laurel. Some of the berries were bigger than the end of Iroquois' thumb. He grinned at his boy, laid down his rifle, and bent to gather the delicacy into a sack he produced from his hunting bag.

A huge black bear rose on its hind legs from the opposite side of the shadowy berry patch. It had been too busy feasting on sweet fruit to notice the hunters' stealthy approach. The startled bruin snarled and frothed and bared its teeth at Bucky and Iroquois who had cornered it against the block of granite. A roar exploded from its five hundred-pound frame, and its fur bristled with rage. With no place to retreat, it dropped to all fours and charged the trespassers, fury blazing in its dark eyes.

Bucky saw his father did not have time to dodge or draw his knife. With three lightning bounds the bear closed on Iroquois, its foul breath blanketing the air. The beast made one final lunge, when a sudden blast filled the quiet grove. Red-hot smoke singed Iroquois' scalp lock, and the bear collapsed in mid-stride to snap and thrash and snarl. It took all the hunter's agility to leap free of the creature's death throes.

Bucky stood five feet behind his father, a smoking rifle still at his shoulder. He figured he had done the right thing, but now his lips quivered as he watched the life ebb out of the giant bruin. He tried hard to keep his hands from shaking. He didn't want Iroquois to see how frightened he really was.

The man's hard face relaxed for a second. Rubbing the back of his scorched neck, he said, "That were a dandy shot, Son. I reckon you saved my life. Even if you did almost ketch me on fire."

Bucky lowered his rifle, and his whole body began to quake. "I'm sorry, Pa," he mumbled. "If I didn't shoot . . . that bear was gonna kill ya! I 'bout took your head off, too. Just a couple inches . . ."

The man's face hardened again. "Sorry for what? It was him or me. Come on. We got a job ahead of us."

It took all of the man and boy's strength to roll the huge bear over on its back and gut it. The young hunter wiped clean his knife blade, and his father said, "This is one fine creature. Its meat will feed us for months, and its fur will make warm winter blankets. I'm proud of how ya nailed him in the forehead. Any other shot woulda never stopped him in time."

The boy smiled at the unexpected compliment. Since Ma had died, there weren't many of those. She had tamed Iroquois, changed him from a trapper who lived with the local Indians to the pa Bucky loved and missed. Now he was a hard man, grunting out instructions like a sullen, old chief. The narrow escape from the bear had loosened his tongue, and the boy was thankful for his father's brief return to his old self.

The hunter grinned back at his son and then muttered with his usual glumness, "I hope you learned what happens when you corner a bear. After we pinned him against the rocks, he had no choice but to charge us."

Bucky shuddered, reliving the sudden, ferocious attack of the snarling bruin. The memory of those huge claws and snapping teeth still filled him with dread. What if his rifle had misfired? What if he had panicked and run? Even worse, what if? . . . Bucky loved hunting with his father, and he had so much to learn from him about guns, the woods, and life. Losing Iroquois was unthinkable, and Bucky's throat tightened when he croaked, "I . . . I . . . I'm just happy we escaped, Pa. How'd we know that nasty fellow was back there? We come on him so quick, and he was nigh onto invisible in them shadows."

"That ain't no excuse. I should have done more scoutin' and less gawkin' at them blueberries."

"But, Pa, you was almost taken. Ma's gone. How would I . . ."

"Come on, boy, let's get haulin'. We still got plenty to do," Iroquois shot back.

"Ah-h-h-h! Can't we rest first, Pa? That bear is so heavy! Just guttin' him's got me all tuckered out. Maybe we could cut him up tomorrow."

"Bucky, you know better than that. We can't leave all that meat here overnight. Wolves would get it fer sure. Now quit your whinin' and give me a hand. It'll take two trips to get the meat back to the cabin. We'll hang the hide in a tree an' fetch it later."

The father and son began the hard work of butchering the great beast. They skinned it, hacked it into quarters, and packed it on their backs across four miles of rough trail. The trail led through the best possible cover for animals and fowl. There were tangles of brush for the grouse; groves of hickory, red oak, and horse chestnut for squirrels and deer; and dark rooms of hemlock for the roosting turkeys. Everywhere the deer had runs trampled into the earth, and the turkeys left their telltale scratches.

By the time the hunters made their second trip, the sun was sinking behind the tall hemlocks. They struggled mightily as they trudged up a steep grade toward the sweetwater spring that bubbled ice cold near their cabin. Finally, the boy cried, "Hold up, Pa! I got a cramp!"

Iroquois helped Bucky take off his pack and sat him down on some mossy rocks next to the spring. Kneading the soreness from his son's muscles, he said, "I can see yer ma in ya, boy. You got her grit, too. She was a good woman."

"Yeah, I remember."

"She thought so much of ya, she called ya Clarence Culp after her grandpap."

"Really, Pa?"

"Yep! But jess the same, I figgered you'd live up to the name I give ya."

"What do you mean?"

"Bucky was my blood brother. He saved my life some years back, just like you did today. Lost him same time you lost yer ma. But now his name will live on with another brave woodsman."

"I . . . I . . . I don't know what to say," choked the boy. "Other than I'm real glad I shot that bear . . . I-I-It's almost dark . . . I guess I can go on now."

Groaning beneath their heavy loads, the hunters hoisted themselves stiffly to their feet. Night was falling fast, and they tramped around a final bend in the trail. Through a gap in the trees, they could just make out the outline of their cabin. It was little more than a windowless shack built of notched logs chinked with mud. It had a dirt floor that froze moccasined feet in the winter and cooled bare toes in July. A crudely mortared fireplace took up the whole back wall. Embers glowed there all hours of the day and night every season of the year.

Bucky and his pa lugged their packs to the root cellar they had dug in the hillside behind the cabin. They creaked open the heavy door and piled their loads of meat carefully inside.

"First thing tomorrow we'll cure this here bear flesh," grunted Iroquois. "Some of it we'll salt. The rest we'll dry in the sun, like always."

Bucky nodded drowsily and followed his father inside their shack. He dropped his empty pack inside the door, leaned his rifle in the corner, and piled wood on the hot fireplace coals. Then, without another word, he collapsed on his pine bough bed and would have immediately fallen into a deep sleep if Iroquois had not snarled, "Ain't you forgittin' somethin', boy? We got guns to clean."

With a groan Bucky crawled to his feet. He was so tired from skinning and hauling the big bear, he could hardly lift his rifle, let alone clean it. But he also knew that although his pa was lax in sweeping out the cabin or washing his soiled buckskins, he would never allow the family weapons to go untended after a day's hunt. As he had witnessed that morning, their very survival depended on their guns being in good working order.

Bucky fetched his thirty caliber Kentucky rifle from the corner and plopped wearily in front of the fireplace next to Iroquois, who sat examining his more powerful forty-five caliber gun. Although Bucky had seen how his rifle could stop a charging bear at point-blank range, he also realized it was better suited for squirrels and turkeys. It fired a single ball that was accurate up to two hundred yards, but lately it had been getting hard to load. Now this really worried him, and he grumbled to his pa, "Why don't my ramrod go all the way down the barrel no more? It's gettin' really bothersome."

"Sounds like black powder is caked in the breech," replied Iroquois. "It's time we take care of that. Pick up yer gun and unpin the barrel from the fore end of the stock."

Iroquois watched Bucky struggle for a moment before demonstrating on his own weapon. Then he continued, "Unhook the tang screw in the rear. No! Like this! Now, carefully remove the breech plug."

After Bucky did as he was instructed, Pa showed him how to ram a water-soaked cloth down the barrel, followed by three pieces of clean cloth. "Now, hold the barrel up to the fire an' peer through it," Iroquois commanded. "If it shines like sun off an elk's antlers, it's clean. If it don't, do it again."

Once Bucky's barrel was unfouled, he mimicked his father by wiping down the outside of his weapon with an oily rag to keep rust from forming on the barrel, hammer, and trigger. He refilled his powder horn and checked his hunting bag to make sure he had enough percussion caps and lead balls for the next day's hunt.

Again Bucky set his gun in the corner and stumbled toward his pine bough bed.

"Ain't you forgittin' somethin' else?" grunted the man from where he squatted next to the fire.

"I don't think so, Pa."

"Didn't I learn you to reload yer gun before puttin' it away?"

"Sorry, Pa."

"Sorry ain't good enough if a wolf or panther busts in here. Ain't you heared 'em prowlin' around our door after sundown?"

"I heared 'em."

"An' if somethin' should bust in here, be sure to make yer first shot count. Aim proper an' squeeze the trigger. Don't forgit that it takes nigh onto a minute to reload a Kentuck rifle. What if you'da missed that chargin' bear? He'da ripped me a new nose hole fer sure. Don't forgit it. Ever!"

Inspired by the memory of that near-death experience, Bucky was quick to take his father's advice to heart. With his fast reflexes and sharp eyes, he learned how to drop a running doe with one shot through the neck or to shoot a posing squirrel through the ear hole at a hundred paces. By the time he reached the age of twelve, he knew he was a first-rate sharpshooter, almost the equal of his teacher.

Chapter Two

THE RENDEZVOUS

The spring Bucky turned twelve, his pa said one night at supper, "I think it's time you come with me to Smethport for the big rendezvous."

"Really, Pa?"

"We caught a powerful number of muskrat an' beaver last winter, an' I need you to help lug them furs into town. It's a good ten-mile hike. Better turn in early, 'cause we'll be leavin' at daybreak."

The next morning Bucky and Iroquois gobbled cold venison for breakfast, shouldered their heavy packs, and headed down the trail for the annual gathering of merchants and trappers at the McKean County seat. It had rained every day for a week, and the deer path they followed had turned into a quagmire. The footing was so slick that Bucky fell again and again in the first mile.

"Sorry I'm slowin' you down, Pa," Bucky said when his father helped him up for the fifteenth time.

"Ain't no matter, boy. I reckon Smethport won't be goin' nowhere."

Finally, Iroquois hacked down a cherry sapling and made a walking stick for his son. Even then, Bucky had trouble fording the rivulets that roared down each gully. Iroquois carried the furs and his son across the largest of these torrents.

It was late morning by the time Bucky and Iroquois broke from the woods into the outskirts of Smethport. There, lining the road into the village, stretched the crude tables and canvas canopies of the outdoor market. Behind each table stood a wisecracking vendor who shouted out a list of his wares. Iroquois pretended to ignore their summons while he sized up each trader in turn. Finally, he swaggered up to a gray-haired geezer whose specialty was beaver traps.

Bucky stared in awe when Iroquois held up a huge pelt and barked, "What'll you give me for this here beaver plew?"

"How 'bout a skinnin' knife?" grunted the merchant.

"Why, that hide come from a seventy-pound male. It's worth twice that puny cutter. And look at that cheap-made handle. Bet that dang blade won't hold an' edge fer five seconds."

"What do you mean?" hissed the geezer. "I carry the best goods in all of western Pennsylvany."

"Hey, you ain't dealin' with no savage here, mister. You can't pawn off no trinkets an' beads on me. I'm offerin' you a prime plew, an' I expect a good re-turn."

"Well, how 'bout two steel beaver traps, then?"

"I might take three of them traps. That is if you throws in that knife for my lad here. Guess it don't look so cheap-made, after all."

"Oh, all right," the seller groaned, handing the knife to the beaming boy.

Bucky examined the stag-handled beauty and then grinned gratefully at his father. This was the first present he had received since his ma's death, and it was anything but flawed as Iroquois had claimed while haggling for it. The knife felt perfectly balanced in the boy's hand. Its five-inch blade was fashioned from tempered steel and was sharp enough to penetrate the toughest hide. Finally, Bucky blurted, "Thank you, Pa. I ain't never seed such a dandy knife as this!"

"I figured I owed you somethin' fer savin' my bacon last fall," said Iroquois with a wink. "Shouldn't have no trouble guttin' the next bear you drop."

Still admiring his treasure, Bucky shadowed Iroquois as he moved from vendor to vendor, swapping his muskrat and beaver pelts for horns of gunpowder, pigs of lead, tin boxes of percussion caps, a hatchet, and an awl. These were the supplies they would need to survive another year, and Iroquois delighted in skinning all the merchants he could while obtaining these essential items.

Iroquois had several pelts left when he stopped in front of a tavern and said, "I'm headin' inside for a little nip, Bucky. You go out in the woods yonder an' cache our supplies. Be sure an' hide 'em good. Meet you back here 'round sundown."

Bucky concealed his pa's purchases and then roamed about Smethport gawking at the brick courthouse, the painted frame houses, and the assorted businesses built along the East West Road. It was his first trip to town, and he marveled at the buildings that towered four stories above him. He was equally amazed by the suits of some of the townsmen. He had always worn clothes made of animal skins, and he wondered how anyone could stay warm in such thin garments.

The village was flooded with rambunctious hunters and trappers who caused one uproar after another. Liquor flowed like the rain-swollen creeks, and Bucky soon learned that brawls were as commonplace as beavers in a ten-acre pond. These men hunted hard and partied the same. Sometimes their parties turned into quarrels and were decided with knives. Usually, though, knives were used in throwing contests that followed shooting contests and wrestling contests and beer-chugging contests and salamander-racing contests.

To Bucky, the most interesting contest of all involved rattlesnakes. The liquor-crazed trappers dumped a bag of vipers into a small pen and then laid down wagers on which of them could edge the closest to the coiled snakes without getting bitten! Bucky cheered on the daring men who defied the buzz and whiplash strike of the deadly rattlers for a few pennies and the rude congratulations of their fellow crazies.

One drunk contestant slipped trying to leap away from a striking rattler and got nailed in the backside. The unlucky fellow squirmed and writhed on the ground until the designated snake doctor peeled off his breeches, cut X's over the twin fang marks, sucked out the poison, and spit it distastefully on the ground. Then the patient swilled medicinal whiskey while waiting for the excruciating stomach spasms and vomiting that were sure to follow.

Bucky laughed at one grizzled, old woodsman who claimed he'd been bitten so many times that he was immune to the venom. He sported a snakeskin band on his weathered hat and cackled like a maniac whenever a rattler would rap him with its fangs.

"That old coot is crazier than an outhouse rat!" screamed one bystander.

"Or he's wearin' leather leggins under his red long johns," jeered his partner.

After Bucky left the rattlesnake contest, he happened upon a pack of boys beating up on a chipmunk-cheeked little fellow dressed in a gray tweed suit and striped stockings. They were taunting him, mussing his hair, and pushing him repeatedly into the mud. The attackers were dirty-faced ruffians who were clad in grubby overalls and faded flannel shirts. They hit their victim from all sides, just like wolves. When they began to rip the sissy's suit, Bucky snarled and lunged at the biggest boy in the pack. With a flurry of punches he bloodied the bully's nose and dropped him yipping like a wounded mongrel into a puddle of cold slop. When Bucky whirled to face the other antagonists, he found them already in mid-flight down an alley. The bully, meanwhile, spun to his feet and exploded in a sprint that sprayed mud in all directions. Bucky's victory whoop harried him until he was out of sight.

Bucky helped the fat-cheeked boy to his feet and handed him his crushed hat. He marveled at how girlish the fellow's features were. He also wondered how someone could gut a deer or lug rocks from a vegetable garden dressed in such a frilly suit. Neither could he understand how a boy could bawl in plain sight of the whole town. Bucky had never allowed himself to cry, not even the time he had stepped in a beaver trap and sprained his foot.

Finally, the little boy composed himself enough to squeak, "How can I ever thank you?"

Startled by the meekness of the kid's voice, Bucky stared numbly without a reply.

"My name is Jimmy Jewett."

Bucky still did not respond until the boy held out his hand and gave his rescuer a weak handshake. Bucky nodded, grunted, and turned to tramp away down the street. He hadn't taken more than five steps, however, before he felt a tug at his sleeve. "Hey, you still haven't told me your name."

"Bucky."

"Boy, Bucky! You sure laid a licking on those fellows. Where are you off to in such a hurry?"

"No place."

"Then let me buy you a treat."

"No."

"Ah, come on. I owe you."

"What for? You was in trouble. I helped. That's it."

Before Bucky could protest again, Jimmy grabbed his arm and pulled him toward the Smethport general store. Inside, next to the counter, there were three wooden pails, each filled with a different kind of candy. There was rock candy, green and red sugar candy, and orange lollipops.

"Go ahead," said Jimmy, motioning toward the three buckets. "Take what you want."

"Ain't there no maple sugar candy?"

"No."

"Then, you pick."

"Give us two lollipops," Jimmy said to the grocer.

"You bet, Jimmy!" the man replied with a wink. "Shall I put it on your family's bill, as usual?"

"Yes, sir, Mister Hamlin."

Bucky and Jimmy licked the suckers and strolled down the East West Road, watching woodsmen barter and curse and guzzle whiskey out of brown jugs. When they stopped awhile to observe a shooting contest, Jimmy said, "How did you like your lollipop?"

"Okay."

"Are you still hungry?"

"I guess so."

"Then why don't you come to my house, and I'll introduce you to my folks."

"I don't know."

"Come on!"

Jimmy boxed Bucky on the shoulder and pointed toward a two-story, white frame house that nestled at the end of the block in a grove of maples.

"You live there?" gasped Bucky. "That's the biggest house on the whole street! Your pa must be rich."

"Nah, it's not ours. It's a parsonage, a church house. Just wait until you see the inside!"

Jimmy broke into a trot toward home, and Bucky, burning with curiosity, rushed along beside him. The boys scurried up a wooden walk and swung open a door constructed of heavy oak. Bucky squinted when they entered a brightly lit foyer. He gasped again while his eyes moved about a sitting room filled with polished furniture and framed family portraits.

Jimmy's mother sat in the far corner playing a spinet. In her long dress and waterfall hairdo, to Bucky she looked like an angel his own ma had described when he was a tad. "Who's your new friend?" she asked in an airy voice.

"Mother, I'd like you to meet Bucky. He just saved my skin."

"Jimmy! What happened? Are you all right? Look at your new suit. Why, the pockets are ripped, and you're muddy from head to foot. How am I ever going to get those trousers clean? Who did this to you?"

"That bully, Bart, and his gang. Bart would have hurt me real bad if Bucky hadn't lit into him and sent him packing with a bloody nose."

"Why, Bucky, aren't you a brave fellow," gushed Mrs. Jewett, as the young woodsman's face turned crimson through his tan. "I don't normally approve of violence, but I'm very glad you saved my son."

Mrs. Jewett continued to sing Bucky's praises until Jimmy's father came in from the kitchen to see who was visiting. Mr. Jewett, a Methodist minister, greeted Bucky with an eloquence the boy had previously encountered only in the shape of a turkey gobbler. Although tall and frail, the preacher's firm handshake and steadfast eyes spoke of an inner strength that made Bucky like him right away. The boy didn't understand much of what Jimmy's father said, but he listened respectfully and bowed his head while the minister offered a prayer of thanks for Bucky's deliverance of Jimmy. "You'll break bread with us, won't you, son?" asked Mr. Jewett.

"Yes, do," said Jimmy's mother. "A guest for dinner is always a delight."

"Come on!" pleaded Jimmy, and Bucky found himself nodding shyly to accept the invitation.

At dinner that evening, Bucky was treated to a sumptuous feast of baked ham, sweet potatoes, and apple pie—none of which he'd eaten since living only with his pa. He also had forgotten how to use silverware. After Jimmy's father said grace, Bucky started cramming the delicious fare into his mouth with his fingers, when Mrs. Jewett froze him with an unapproving frown. "Didn't your mother teach you table manners?" she asked gently.

"My ma is dead," blurted Bucky.

"Oh, I'm so sorry."

Jimmy stared at Bucky aghast, but Mr. Jewett simply said, "Eat with this, Bucky," and demonstrated the polite use of the fork. When Bucky drew his new skinning knife to cut his meat, again Mr. Jewett intervened with, "No, son, use the knife next to your plate."

Once Bucky began eating in a civilized manner, Mrs. Jewett again favored him with a smile. "This is the first time I've seen you here in Smethport," she said. "Did you just move here with your family?"

"No, ma'am. I live with my pa out in our hollow."

"Don't you have any brothers and sisters?"

"No. Just me and Pa."

"Do you have a farm?"

"No."

"Then how do you live?"

"We hunt. We trap. We eat."

"Oh!"

After supper the little family gathered in the sitting room to chat and sing energetic hymns. Between songs, Bucky answered most questions about himself with a nod or a shy smile, but he loved being the center of attention just the same. He also loved watching Mrs. Jewett play the spinet with her long, delicate fingers. He wondered how she could make such pretty sounds by touching those keys. The kindness of her eyes reminded him so much of his own mother that finally he stood up and stammered, "Thank you for dinner and everything. I gotta go now. To find my pa."

"Oh, you don't have to leave so soon, do you?" asked Jimmy.

Bucky nodded, lowered his eyes, and began to shuffle toward the front door. Mr. Jewett intercepted him in the hall and shook hands. His wife gave Bucky a motherly hug. "Don't make yourself a stranger," she said.

Stepping into the damp evening air, Bucky felt strangely aglow from the hot meal and the family's display of affection. He smiled to himself, mindful of all the wonderful things he had seen that day. He had just begun whistling a happy tune when a giant paw slammed down on his shoulder and spun him in a half circle.

Bucky found himself face-to-face with an enraged mountain of a man. He had a black beard that hung down to his waist and a full head of black hair that cascaded from beneath a slouch hat often worn by lumberjacks. His arms were easily the size of Bucky's thighs, and his red pig eyes were swollen from alcohol and tobacco smoke.

"I finally found you, you little weasel," boomed the giant. "You're the Injun that beat up on my boy!"

"What do you mean, mister?" wheezed Bucky, trying hard to hide his trembling.

"You know what I mean!" the ruffian howled and yanked Bucky off his feet. "My boy's got a busted nose. He says you done it. Says you blindsided him. Now you're gonna pay!"

When the bruin-sized man raised his other fist to smash Bucky, the boy hammered the logger's sensitive snout until he released his grip. Before the giant could recover, Bucky dodged beyond his reach and hightailed it down the street. Although the lumberjack bellowed every obscenity known to McKean County, the boy easily outdistanced him and disappeared down the same alley where the man's son had made his escape.

Bucky ran until his mouth tasted like copper and his vision blurred from sweat. Finally, in front of the courthouse he slipped, panting, beneath a thorny hedge to hug the ground and quiet the pounding in his temples. His lungs rasped like an overworked bellows. His legs quivered in spasms of fright.

Minutes later, the thud of the boy's pulse kept him from hearing the whisper of footsteps slipping through the shadows. It wasn't until the bushes rustled just above his head that Bucky became aware of the red pig eyes probing the hedge for him.

"Gotcha now!" thundered the giant, fishing through the bushes with his ham hands.

Bucky wormed away just as the man reached to snatch him.

"Come back here, you! I'm gonna skin you alive!"

With a yelp, Bucky exploded from the hedge, sprinted down a side street, and hurdled two fences before the giant could disentangle himself from the prickly bushes. The boy never quit running until he found his pa slumped outside the Bennett House Hotel. Pa was too soused to ask what was the matter, and Bucky didn't volunteer any information about the thorn scratches that crisscrossed his face.

Chapter Three

HUNTING AND FORAGING

While Bucky hunted and foraged for food that spring, he often thought of his experiences in town. Clumsy fawns clambering up a creek bank reminded him of Jimmy, while in a pair of feuding bear cubs he saw two trappers wrestling for a rendezvous prize. Even the growls of the mother bear made him think of Smethport. Closing his eyes, Bucky recollected how the tangle-bearded giant made a similar sound when reaching to snatch him from the courthouse hedge. He made these observations from the safety of an oak tree, remembering well his lesson on cornered bruins.

Although food was again plentiful, nothing Bucky ate could compare with the delicious dinner Mrs. Jewett had prepared that night in town. A pot of boiled cowslips or leeks tasted downright tame next to sweet potatoes. Even a grouse cooked on a spit paled in comparison to baked ham. "Ain't we gettin' perticular," snapped Iroquois one night when Bucky refused a strip of deer loin. "You'da give your right arm fer that meat last winter."

April turned to May, and the creeks warmed enough for the brook trout to begin actively feeding. One warm, sunny afternoon Bucky yelled, "Goin' fishin', Pa," and headed for his favorite trout stream. When he caught his first glimpse of the shimmering brook, he stopped along the trail and cut a sapling for a fishing pole. To the end of his pole, he tied a length of string and attached a stone sinker. He had no metal hooks. Instead, he threaded a worm on a piece of twig knotted on his line.

Bucky crawled on all fours to the edge of a long, deep pool and cast stealthily upstream. When a sleek trout darted from beneath an undercut bank and took the bait, Bucky allowed the fish time to swallow it. Tightening the line lodged the twig sideways in the brookie's throat, and he soon hauled the squirming fish out of the water. Fishing the bottom of still holes brought the best results that time of year. In an hour he caught so many trout, he had a hard time carting them all home.

In May the turkey gobblers did their mating dance to impress their flocks of females. They preened and strutted and even ran to a concealed hunter who called like a lovesick hen. The next morning Bucky hid in a windfall and made clucking noises by rubbing a fire-hardened stick on a piece of slate. This was nerve-racking work, for once a bearded tom puffed out its feathers and swaggered into view, Bucky dared not move until he had a clear shot. Even mating turkeys had the keenest eyesight in the forest. One premature twitch of a head or finger would send a gobbler scrambling for cover or flush him into the air.

Bucky worked his call until he heard flapping wings coming toward him through the trees. Instinctively he froze in place, and within seconds, turkeys glided from the sky and landed all around him. There were so many hens and gobblers scurrying through the brush that Bucky had a hard time deciding which one to shoot. Finally, he trained his sights on a big gobbler running straight away from him and squeezed off a steady shot. The bullet tore through the center of the bird and flattened it in mid-stride just before it leaped down a gully.

Bucky jumped to his feet, whooped in jubilation, and hurdled several deadfalls in his mad rush to retrieve his kill.

Hoisting the big tom with his right hand, he shouted, "Whew, look at that six-inch beard!"

The bird weighed over twenty pounds, and Bucky admired its big, bluish head and wrinkled, red neck. At a distance, turkeys always appeared black in color, but up close this one's feathers had a greenish bronze sheen that reminded him of the ceremonial Indian garb Iroquois once wore when he visited his former tribe.

Bucky slung the bird over his shoulder and started down the trail to the cabin. He hadn't taken more than a few steps when his pa hastened through the brush toward him. "I was goin' to ask if ya saw them turkeys I kicked out over yonder, but I might as well save my breath," puffed Iroquois with an envious glance at Bucky's big tom.

"I wondered where they come from," replied the boy. "For awhile I thought it was rainin' turkeys when they begun lightin' on the ground."

"That's a mighty nice bird ya got there. We'll roast him up for supper. Now, though, we gotta head back and work on the garden if we wants anything besides fowl and venison to eat."

"Ah, Pa! Do we have to?" Bucky asked, but he already knew the answer.

Iroquois led his son back down the mountain to the clearing they had axed from an oak grove next to their shack. After Bucky had plucked and cleaned his turkey, he helped his father gouge rocks from the glacier-gutted soil. Each spring new stones pressed to the surface and had to be cleared away. Iroquois had started to build a fence with them six years ago, and it now stretched halfway around the side yard.

Iroquois swung a homemade hoe while Bucky worked a wooden shovel to break up the clods of sod and clay. Corn, squash, and beans were all that would grow in this poor soil. Like his Seneca Indian brothers, Iroquois buried fish to fertilize his crop. He also got the seeds he needed from his former tribe. Tilling this garden was backbreaking work, but the vegetables that escaped the coons and rabbits were a welcome change from wild game.

Working the garden was doubly tough in June when the gnats and black flies harassed both man and beast. At the height of the hatch, a swarm of insects descended upon Bucky and his father the moment they left the cabin with their tools. They tried daubing mud on their exposed skin to deter the blood-thirsty insects. Finally, Bucky threw down his shovel and howled, "These pesky critters just won't quit bitin', Pa."

"I reckon you're right, boy," grunted Iroquois. "Let's git back inside while we still got some hide left on us!"

July and August were lazy months for Bucky and Iroquois. The only real work they had was weeding and watering the garden. The rest of the day they lounged barefoot in the shade to escape the heat. When they were hungry, it was easy enough to shoot a browsing deer within a few hundred yards of the cabin. Sometimes Bucky wouldn't even have to leave the yard to get supper. All he had to do was wait with his slingshot near their vegetable patch and pick off one of the rabbits that appeared around dusk.

Often, to break the monotony of summer, Bucky hunted bullfrogs that thrived in several beaver ponds just down the valley. He sneaked along the brushy shore of these impoundments listening for the croakers' bass voices. They were usually hard to spot because they floated with just their greenish yellow heads protruding from the brackish water. Bucky had tried spearing and netting the slippery amphibians, but they always dove from danger. One day the young woodsman lunged forward with his net, lost his balance, and toppled into the deep, sucking pond muck. If he hadn't snatched hold of some overhanging branches, he surely would have drowned. After that, he took his Kentucky rifle to the marshes with him and carted home a bag of delicious frog legs to cook in the iron skillet.

"Them legs taste just like chicken," Iroquois said, smacking his lips.

"I'll have to take your word for it, Pa. I ain't never ate any tame fowl."

Of all the seasons, Bucky loved early autumn best. Then he and his pa gorged themselves on berries, ripe fruit, cooked vegetables, and luscious mushrooms. It was during this time that foraging even took precedence over hunting, and they tried to fill their root cellar with enough apples to last them at least until December. Often at harvest time Iroquois would make a trip to a local farm to trade for potatoes. These, too, could be stored well into the winter when hunting became fruitless if not altogether impossible.

To Bucky, winter was longer than the other three seasons combined. With snow drifted up around the cabin, there wasn't much to do but sleep and stay warm. He and his pa took turns checking their trap line or skinning the animals snared. Sometimes that took half a day. Other times they sewed fringed shirts and leggings from cured deer hide. Usually, though, their waking hours were spent staring into the fire. Bucky often wished he could live in a grand house like Jimmy. Only when he remembered the pretty music played by Mrs. Jewett, did the four walls of the tiny cabin not close in so tightly.

Being cooped up with an untalkative man like Pa didn't make the winter pass any faster, either. Iroquois just wasn't much for local yarns or gossip, and he seldom spoke of himself or his past. Bucky knew his father escaped by thinking about Ma. When Iroquois' hawklike eyes lapsed into a catatonic trance, his spirit was off someplace visiting the love of his life.

Chapter Four

JIMMY'S SCHOOL

While Bucky was huddled in the cabin all winter trying to stay warm, Jimmy was following a much more structured routine in Smethport. Every weekday morning the preacher's son awoke at first light and immediately scrambled into his neatly pressed school clothes. Then he hurried downstairs to gobble the eggs his mother faithfully prepared for him. After Mrs. Jewett helped him on with his coat and hat, he bolted out the door toward the one-room schoolhouse across town.

Jimmy always left for school a half-hour earlier than his classmates. His survival depended upon it. Weighted down by his lunch and heavy books, it took him at least twenty minutes to trudge through the snowy streets to safety. He glanced fearfully into every alley he passed and often thought of the "valley of the shadow of death" he had read about in Psalm 23.

When Jimmy arrived at school, he rushed to his front row desk and got out his completed homework. He always had his lessons prepared, and his teacher, Miss Dempsey, smiled her approval while she wrote the day's assignments on the blackboard. Jimmy sat as close to her as possible so he wouldn't miss one word of her lectures. He was especially interested in the talks she gave on America's founding fathers and the Constitution. They were so inspiring that Jimmy learned to recite the Preamble by heart and then memorized the Bill of Rights.

"Mr. Jewett, why are you so fascinated by the workings of our government?" his teacher asked one day after Jimmy had interrupted her lecture to inquire about the system of checks and balances provided by the Constitution.

"Well, ma'am, I was thinking about studying law someday."

"Isn't that wonderful!" blared Miss Dempsey. "How would you like me to tutor you in Latin after school? Latin is a subject all lawyers must master."

"Why, thank you, ma'am. That's very kind of you. I'll have to ask my mother first."

Of course, Miss Dempsey's kind offer didn't make Jimmy any more popular with his classmates. Like Bart, the bully, they were mainly the sons of loggers or farmers and only saw school as a temporary escape from their heavy chores. Most of them had to be browbeaten by the teacher to learn to write their names and do simple ciphering, and it rankled them that little Jimmy Jewett was always extending her already long-winded discussions. These boys would do little more with their lives than plow up the earth or hack down trees. They only listened to the nonsense spewing out of Miss Dempsey's mouth because otherwise they would have a book chucked at their heads or would get rapped with a yardstick. Jimmy Jewett was the only kid in the class who didn't nightly carry home welts meted out by the iron-fisted schoolmarm for speaking out of turn or starting a test prematurely. Now that he was to receive private tutoring, he became even more hated by Bart and the others.

After their history, reading, and spelling lessons, the students were dismissed for lunch, and everyone but Jimmy returned home for a hot meal. Jimmy carried his lunch because he knew if he left the schoolhouse the other boys would be waiting to steal his mittens, push him into snowdrifts, and fill his hat with slush. Instead of putting himself through that every day, he huddled by the potbellied stove and ate the bag of food his mother packed for him. Lately, though, his lunch had gotten skimpier and skimpier. First, apples disappeared from the paper sack. Next, it was cheese. Finally, even the slices of homemade bread got thinner.

Miss Dempsey always stayed during the noon hour to correct papers, and sometimes Jimmy helped her check the other boys' spelling. The woman was big-built with fleshy biceps and bright red hair. She also had a ruddy complexion that flamed bright crimson when someone set off her Irish temper. Her students, though, whispered her skin color was due to the bottle of mythical whiskey she had stashed in her desk. Although she barked like a lumber crew foreman even when engaged in private conversation, Jimmy was thankful for her company—and protection.

During lunch one sunny February day, Miss Dempsey said to Jimmy, "Why don't you go outside and enjoy the sun? It might be the only time it shines this whole month. This is one devil of a winter. I swear I've never seen so many bleak, snowy days."

"If it's all the same to you, ma'am," replied Jimmy, "I'd rather stay here. I . . . have to work some more on my long division."

"Do you want me to send notes home to the fathers of those boys who are picking on you, Mr. Jewett?"

"But that would be almost everyone in the class," blurted Jimmy.

"I know. What if I were to say something to them?"

"N-o-o-o! That would only make things worse."

"Well, you can't go on hiding in here forever. Sooner or later they're going to hurt you if something isn't done."

That very afternoon, after Jimmy finished his Latin lesson, he found a gang of boys waiting in ambush for him in an alley just off the school grounds. As he stumbled past the town tavern, his assailants emerged from their hiding place to fling a volley of heavy slush balls. One icy projectile laid open Jimmy's cheek while another cracked the lenses of his spectacles. The blows to the face bowled him over backwards, spilling his books onto the frozen road. Before he could regain his feet, the bully Bart stood over him, filling the street with mocking laughter.

"Where's yer Injun friend this time?" Bart crowed. "Now we're gonna stomp ya good!"

"Yeah!" snarled another boy. "See how many questions ya ask that witch Dempsey with a busted jaw."

"Then, we're gonna knock yer teeth down yer throat," promised Bart. "That'll keep ya from whinin' about us to yer mommy."

Jimmy squinted through the cracked lenses at the scowling bully and his pack of posturing confederates. They stood with their chests thrust forward and their hands clenched into fists. They wore slouch hats and dyed wool jackets. Hatred turned their eyes as glassy as if they'd guzzled a tumbler of corn whiskey.

After Jimmy wiped the blood from his cheek, a sudden surge of fear propelled him forward on all fours. The bullies stared in amazement when he squirmed through their maze of legs and took off running toward home. With a curse, Bart whirled to lead his howling henchmen in a dead gallop after the preacher's boy.

Jimmy ran like a spooked gelding for two blocks, kicking up snow and skidding on ice. His jacket flared behind him while his arms pumped and his pudgy legs struggled to keep pace. He had almost outdistanced his tormentors when he slipped on the slick street in front of the Bennett House. Somehow he kept his legs flailing until he regained his balance and shot off again past the general store. Half of Bart's buddies, however, weren't so lucky. Their feet flew out from under them, and they fell heavily on their backs to squirm and kick and swear.

Jimmy could hear Bart's labored breathing grow ever closer as he rushed up the wooden walk to his house. Once, the bully's fingers closed on his jacket before pulling free at Jimmy's renewed burst of speed. The boy ripped open the door and ducked inside just in time to evade Bart's final lunge. The ruffian smacked head-on into the closing panel of oak and had to be dragged away by his still-cursing gang.

"What in the world?" asked Mrs. Jewett when her gasping son burst into the sitting room. "What's wrong with you, Jimmy? You act like you're being chased by the devil himself."

Jimmy collapsed exhausted on the rug. Blood dribbled down his cheek, and his smashed spectacles sat lopsided on his puffy nose. His mother took one look at his gory countenance and shrieked, "Father, get down here! Now!"

Reverend Jewett rushed down the stairs with the pages of his latest sermon clutched in his hand. "Are you all right, son?" he gasped. "What happened to your face? And your glasses?"

"I . . . I . . . I was outrunning . . . a stray dog. I tripped . . . and broke them."

"Oh, dear!" exclaimed Mrs. Jewett, wiping Jimmy's face with a damp rag. "Was the mongrel foaming at the mouth?"

"N-o-o-o."

"Those sounded like human footsteps to me," corrected the reverend. "I'm sorry, but we won't be able to replace those spectacles right away."

"Why not, Father?"

"Most of our congregation hasn't been able to pay their tithes lately. This winter has been tough on everyone."

"That's right," added Mrs. Jewett. "Brother Wright didn't even bring us any eggs today. We'll have to make due with bread for breakfast."

"How about some blackberry jam?"

"We ran out of that today, too."

"It figures," sighed Jimmy. "This is the worst winter of my whole life!"

Chapter Five

FEEDING THE JEWETTS

The following spring Bucky planned to visit the Jewetts when he and his pa made their annual trip to the Smethport rendezvous. He reminisced all morning about the family's kindness and impatiently waited for his father to finish bartering. His fidgeting got on Iroquois' nerves until the old horse trader snapped, "What ails you, son? Got spiders in your drawers?"

Bucky cached his pa's acquisitions and then made a beeline for the two-story frame house with the wooden walk. He hammered on the oak door until Reverend Jewett answered his knock with a surprised "Hello" and a hearty handshake. Jimmy and his mother boiled out of the kitchen at the sound of Bucky's voice. Jimmy tugged happily on his friend's sleeve while Mrs. Jewett smothered him with motherly hugs.

"Come in! Come in!" invited Jimmy's father. "What have you been doing with yourself all these months?"

"Me and Pa trapped us some huge beaver. The biggest we ever caught."

"Good for you, Bucky!" shouted Jimmy. "I'll bet they brought a good price."

"'Specially the way Pa trades," chuckled Bucky.

"I only wish our winter had gone as well," said Mrs. Jewett sadly.

"What's wrong?" asked Bucky, noting a new thinness to the woman's still beautiful face.

"It was a very harsh winter," said Reverend Jewett. "Our food supply is just about gone."

"Yeah," added Jimmy. "We haven't had much other than potato soup for the last week."

"And you should thank the Lord for that," replied his father. "Many of my parishioners haven't even got that."

"I'm sorry, Father."

"What are you going to do?" asked Bucky with a concerned nod.

"I guess we'll just have to trust in the Lord."

"I have an idea," said Bucky.

"What's that, dear?" asked Mrs. Jewett.

"Let Jimmy come hunting with me, an' we'll see what we can shoot."

"Wouldn't that be dangerous?"

"Ah, Mother!"

After gaining the Jewetts' reluctant consent, Bucky led his friend to his supply cache on the outskirts of town and fetched his rifle, powder horn, and hunting bag. Then he and Jimmy cut into the woods until they struck the first fresh deer path pounded into the forest floor. The young woodsman moved as silently as a moccasined panther, while his village counterpart snapped twigs and crunched leaves with his top boots. Finally, Bucky ordered his friend to remove his boots. Jimmy sputtered in protest until Bucky snarled, "Do you wanna eat, or not?"

The mud squished between his toes as Jimmy shadowed his friend along the deer path. "My mother's going to be awfully upset when she sees my muddy feet. She'll rant about me catching cold, too," he whispered under his breath. He was so wrapped up in his personal fears that he didn't notice that Bucky had stopped until he rammed into him.

Bucky hissed a warning and motioned toward the beech brush on the hillside directly below them. Jimmy stared intently into the screen of burnt orange leaves until his legs cramped from being frozen in an awkward position. He was about to lurch backward to relieve his pain when Bucky eased his rifle to his shoulder and carefully aimed at what must truly be a phantom. The rifle roared and spit fire. Rocked by the explosion, Jimmy covered his ears and collapsed to his knees in fright.

Meanwhile, the young woodsman slipped noiselessly forward, reloading his rifle. He drew a measure of gunpowder from his horn flask and poured it down the barrel. Next, he wrapped a ball in a greased patch and seated it in the barrel with a short starter dowel. After he withdrew the ramrod from the fore end of the stock, he rammed the bullet and patch down on top of the powder charge. He replaced the ramrod, took a percussion cap from the tin in his hunting bag, drew back his hammer to half cock, and placed the cap on the exposed nipple. Uncocking his gun, he skated adroitly down over the bank and disappeared into the thick beech.

Several human hoots echoed from below, and Jimmy crawled shakily to his feet. When the hooting became more urgent, he rolled down over the bank in a shower of mud, sliming himself from head to foot. He was about to burst into tears when Bucky's face appeared in the beech. Snickering at his friend's clumsiness, Bucky motioned for Jimmy to follow.

The boys moved forty yards into the thicket before they came to a huge doe piled up at the base of an oak. Blood was oozing from a neat hole through the center of its neck. Jimmy stared in disbelief and then stammered, "W-W-W-hat the—? H-H-How the—? I didn't see anything!"

"Have to know what to look for," replied Bucky. "First, moving ears . . . A round rump and legs . . . Then, you'll see the whole deer."

Without further explanation, Bucky drew his knife, rolled the doe over on her back, and began slitting open her belly. Jimmy watched until his friend plunged his hands into the chest cavity and began yanking out the entrails. The gagging town boy bent over a log and emptied the contents of his own stomach.

Hungry from the exertion of the hunt, Bucky took some flint and steel from his hunting bag and started a fire by striking sparks into a pile of dry pine twigs. He added bigger twigs and limbs until he was able to cook deer liver on a spit. Bucky gobbled it greedily, while his friend continued to be sick.

With his hunger satisfied, Bucky concealed the remaining liver back in the chest cavity of the huge doe. His neck shot had killed her instantly and had ruined very little meat. He could not understand why Jimmy was upset by the killing of the animal when its death would ensure the survival of his family.

When Bucky had finished admiring his kill, he said a silent prayer to the Indians' Great Spirit and then fetched a stout rope from his hunting bag. He fastened the rope around the doe's neck and began dragging the beast through the brush toward town. It was tough going on bare ground. Often he slipped and fell headlong into the mud. Finally, he asked Jimmy to carry his hunting bag and powder horn. When his friend offered to carry his rifle too, Bucky grunted, "No!"

It took the boys two hours to drag the deer back to Smethport. Carrying firewood was the only physical work ever required of Jimmy. He blistered his girlish hands on the drag rope when Bucky become too exhausted to tug anymore. By the time they reached the East West Road, it took what was left of their combined strength to move Bucky's kill at all. The doe weighed upwards to 130 pounds, and offers were shouted from each meat market the boys dragged the deer past on the way to Jimmy's. One butcher was so desperate for game that he and two of his dark-bearded henchmen would have swiped the big doe had Bucky not threatened them with his rifle and growled like a half-starved dog.

Finally, Bucky and Jimmy pulled the deer into the Jewetts' backyard and collapsed in an unmoving heap. Jimmy's mother hurried from the porch swing to hover about the boys like a concerned hen. Reverend Jewett soon joined her, carrying torn strips of soft cloth and a wooden bucket of water. He washed Jimmy's feet while his wife applied salve to his blistered hands.

Bucky gulped an offered glass of spring water and sat with his back against a big backyard maple to catch his breath. Then he staggered wearily to his feet to pitch the tow rope over an overhead branch. With all the strength he could muster, he heaved on the rope until even the huge doe's back hooves dangled in the air. With a grunt he tied off the rope to the trunk of the maple and fell to skinning his kill. While the Jewetts watched in awe, Bucky peeled off the hide, using his knife to slice it free from the deer's flesh. The animal had a fine skin that the family could trade for a large supply of flour, sugar, or tea. Once butchered, the meat itself could be canned or dried and would keep the family from starving for the rest of the spring.

After the skinning was finished, Bucky squatted Indian-style against the tree. Mrs. Jewett brought him another glass of water, and after taking a long gulp, he nodded toward the deer and said, "I shot her for you . . . and your family."

Reverend Jewett began to protest until his wife touched his arm and said, "How can we ever thank you, Bucky?" When her grateful smile washed over him, she did more to repay the boy than she ever could have imagined.

By then, Jimmy was back on his feet, shouting, "You should have seen the shot Bucky made on this deer, Father. It was standing in brush so thick I couldn't even see it. Somehow, Bucky hit it right through the neck!"

Mr. Jewett shot his son an unbelieving look when Jimmy added, "It's the honest-to-goodness truth. Look at the bullet hole if you don't believe me."

"However he happened to kill it, we should thank our Heavenly Father for delivering us from our hunger."

"Yes, and for sending us such a good friend," reminded Jimmy.

The young woodsman felt his face turning crimson when Mrs. Jewett added, "We're beholden to you, Bucky. We love you."

Chapter Six

BREWER'S REVENGE

When Bucky returned to the tavern that evening to meet his pa, he found Iroquois lying unconscious in an alley. He reeked of foul rum, and his face was bloody and discolored from what appeared to be a severe beating. How he had gotten in that condition, Bucky didn't wait around to discover. He dragged his pa's body into the shadows of a nearby hotel and ran to fetch Jimmy.

The Jewetts were in the middle of canning venison when Bucky rapped on their back door. "What happened?" asked Mrs. Jewett when she saw the boy's troubled face.

"It's my pa!" he blurted.

"What's wrong with your father?" asked Reverend Jewett.

"He got beat up. Bad! Please let Jimmy come."

"Wouldn't it be better if I came with you?" suggested the minister. "What can Jimmy do?"

"Help me take Pa home."

"But isn't that a long walk from here?"

"Two hours," replied Bucky. "I'll bring Jimmy back tomorrow."

"I've got a better idea," said Mrs. Jewett. "If your father is badly hurt, why don't you bring him here?"

"Oh, I can't let you see Pa . . . like that!"

Reverend Jewett turned to his wife, shook his head, and said to Jimmy, "We'll see you tomorrow."

"Wear your wool coat and hat, young man," shouted Mrs. Jewett before Jimmy disappeared out the door.

Bucky lit out down the East West Road with Jimmy close at his heels. When the boys sprinted up to the Bennett House, where Bucky had left Pa, they could hear a low moan coming from the shadows. Finally, they noticed a dim form slumped near the dark foundation of the hotel.

Iroquois had risen to his knees and was holding his battered face. His right eye had swollen shut, and his nose pointed at an unnatural angle. When the boys approached, he snarled like a wounded cougar and drew his knife from its sheath.

The breath whistled from Jimmy's lungs at his first sight of Iroquois. The scalp lock, the bloody face, the rum-soaked buckskin were all so shocking he would have bolted back home had it not been for his sense of debt to his friend.

"It's me, Pa," Bucky whispered. "Don't you know me? What happened?"

Iroquois growled and spit until finally the calm tone of Bucky's voice led to a sense of recognition. He allowed the boys to hoist him to his feet and lead him stumbling down a shadowy alley until they reached the woods.

Bucky found their supply cache in the dark without a torch or candle. He loaded up Jimmy with four horns of powder, two bulging hunting bags, and two ten-pound Kentucky rifles. This done, he said to Iroquois, "Lean on my shoulder, Pa. I'll get you home."

As the trio staggered up the trail, the moon rose to lend a haunted glow to the foggy forest landscape. Peepers chirped in the marshes. Owls hooted in the hemlock. Wolves howled in the beech. Jimmy's fear intensified with each new voice that joined the terrible chorus. Despite the coolness of the night, he was soon clammy with a noxious sweat that rivaled the reek of rum wafting from Iroquois.

Bucky kept a steady pace for an hour. Although his pa was still dazed from his beating, his feet worked fine once they felt the familiar trail beneath them. It was nothing for him and Bucky to cover thirty miles in a day, so even in a half-zombie state, the trip home from Smethport was easy.

Unfortunately, that was not the case for Jimmy. Clad in his heavy top boots and loaded down with rifles and supplies, he was winded in the first thirty minutes of their journey. He crashed along like a spooked mule tripping over roots and stones. He fell further and further behind the woodsmen until he collapsed halfway up a steep gully.

Bucky was forced to build a fire to revive his father and his friend. While he fed the flames until they licked at the night sky, he chastised Jimmy for dropping the rifles during his fall. Jimmy was too frozen and exhausted to pay any attention. He now looked worse than Iroquois. His pudgy face was ashen hued, and his blue lips shivered uncontrollably. He stared numbly into the flames, afraid to look beyond them.

Iroquois huddled so close to the fire that steam rose from his sweat-soaked clothes. As his brain became less jumbled, he began to reconstruct the evening's events. It wasn't long before he saw visions of giant fists hammering into him. When he winced with the memory, Bucky prodded, "What's wrong, Pa?"

"Just remembered . . . how I got jumped."

"You do?"

"Went outside . . . the Bennett House . . . for some air . . . A huge man . . . bullies me . . . My Indian clothes . . . Says a boy . . . my spittin' image . . . beat up . . . his son . . . last year's . . . rendezvous. He was powerful . . . drunk . . . Punched . . . like a mule . . . Hit me . . . again . . . again . . ."

"Did the man have a tangled, black beard?"

"How did you . . . know?"

"'Cause he's the same fella come after me," confessed Bucky.

"After you?"

"He didn't like the way I run off his boy when I caught him pickin' on Jimmy. Musta decided to get even with you instead of me."

"Dang! You shoulda said somethin', boy."

"You mean Bart's father did this to you?" gasped Jimmy. "Why, he's the worst scoundrel in Smethport. It seems like every time he comes home from logging, he gets drunk and beats someone half to death. And he never forgets an insult."

"I ain't interested in gettin' in no feud," groaned Iroquois. "'Specially with a fella that big. I'm a peaceable man. That's why I moved out to the hollow."

"It won't do any good to go to the constable, either," whined Jimmy. "He's scared of Bart's father, too. Now do you see why I never fight back?"

Bucky swallowed hard and then kicked some dirt on the fire. "I guess we better get movin'," he said. "We still got a ways to go."

Iroquois now was able to hobble along on his own, so Bucky relieved Jimmy of the rifles and powder horns. They all moved better after their rest and traveled on without further incident until they reached Bucky's home woods.

Jimmy's eyes had grown accustomed to the darkness, and he seemed less apprehensive of the nocturnal beasts that bolted through the brush at their passing. His final shock of the night came when he stumbled into the Culps' clearing and caught sight of the crude dwelling that was his friend's home. Bucky would have been deeply hurt if he could have seen the dismay that washed over Jimmy's face when he ducked inside the shack and was told to find a seat on the earthen floor next to Iroquois.

Bucky hung the rifles upside down above the hearth. In a moment a bright fire leaped up the stone chimney, and Jimmy stared owl-eyed at the mud-chinked log walls. A table constructed of rough-hewn lumber sat in the middle of the floor surrounded by stump seats of varying heights. Two piles of hemlock boughs served as beds, and bearskin blankets lay near the hearth. A rude cupboard containing wooden trenchers, wooden eating utensils, and tin percussion cap boxes hung at a crazy angle off one wall. Powder horns hung from pegs on another. The door was hinged by leather straps and secured with a stout wood dowel. Nowhere were there pictures, items of glass, books, or any other sign of civilization. Take away the rifles and the box of steel tools, and the cabin might well have been inhabited by people of the Bronze Age.

Bucky disappeared out the door while Jimmy and Iroquois crawled closer to the fire. He soon returned with a huge armful of fresh pine boughs that masked the sour odor of sweat, damp earth, and old animal skins. He made two more trips into the night until he had three soft beds laid out in front of the hearth. When he had finished, he wrapped himself in a bear skin and was soon sound asleep.

After Iroquois collapsed on his bed, Jimmy continued to stare into the flames flicking up the chimney. He didn't half know what to make of what he had seen that day. His romantic notions of Bucky's life in the wilderness had been shattered, but that didn't make the young woodsman any less his friend.

The next morning Jimmy awoke from a fitful sleep to find Bucky and Iroquois studying him from the table. It was apparent that they had been up for some time, for they were plucking two fat grouse that would be their breakfast. Jimmy was stiff from a night in a pine bough bed, and his legs ached from their recent exertion. When he sat up to watch Bucky roast the birds over the hearth fire, he saw a freshly stitched pair of moccasins lying on the floor next to his heavy top boots.

"They're for you," said Iroquois, as if reading his mind. "Boots ain't no good. Crack too many twigs. Scare game away."

Jimmy tried on his new moccasins after breakfast, and then Bucky took him on a walk through the hollow. Jimmy was amazed at how noiselessly he and his friend slipped along the deer paths that meandered through the woods.

"Pa said to bring back some game for lunch," reminded Bucky after they entered a grove of gnarled oak. "Why don't you see if you can shoot us some?"

"But I don't know anything about guns."

"Don't worry," replied his friend. "I'll show you. All ya gotta do is yank back the hammer, raise the stock to your shoulder, point the bead on the barrel at a critter's head, an' slowly squeeze the trigger. You can do it."

When the boys again began sneaking down the trail, Jimmy was in the lead carrying the rifle. They continued to slink along until he spotted a large gray squirrel poised on an oak trunk not more than twenty-five paces away. He cocked the gun and aimed it like he had been instructed, but the barrel was so heavy it wobbled wildly in a full circle. When he pulled back on the trigger, there was a clap of thunder that made him jump and almost drop the rifle. Just the same, in a moment Bucky returned carrying a fat squirrel drilled through the head.

"Nice shot," chuckled Bucky, giving his friend a playful cuff.

Jimmy rubbed his arm and grinned back. "I wish I could stay longer and learn more about shooting, but my father expects me home today."

"I know. After lunch we'll go back. Then you'll know how to come here anytime you want."

Jimmy smiled at the thought, but he knew that Reverend Jewett would never allow him to go off into the woods by himself. And, of course, he also had school and Miss Dempsey's beloved lectures on the Constitution.

Chapter Seven

Wolves!

The winter of 1860 began with a late October blizzard that made hunting almost impossible. Deer trails disappeared under three-foot drifts as the wind screamed out of the north with lethal ferocity. Snow was up to a man's waist and a deer's belly, which made travel a difficult chore. The laurel and beech thickets were buried, too, and the hemlocks had so much snow pasted on their boughs that a hunter's visibility was limited to twenty or thirty yards. All Bucky and Iroquois could do was hole up in their shack, try to stay warm, and wait for the weather to break.

However, the weather never did break. One squall followed another until the hunters found themselves snowbound. With so much winter engulfing the landscape, the animals simply disappeared. Squirrels hunkered in their nests, grouse burrowed beneath logs, and the deer yarded up in secret thickets. To Bucky it was like the earth had swallowed up all of God's creatures. Even when he went out on snowshoes, he found not a single track or dropping to betray their hiding places.

Bucky and Iroquois had shot a deer the day before the storm hit, and its skinned carcass hung frozen from an oak outside the cabin. In addition, they had pemmican, apples, and a few potatoes Iroquois had bartered for that fall. Bucky also caught an occasional snowshoe rabbit in his snares.

40

With food so scarce, he and his pa decided to cut back to one meal a day.

When the winter became more extreme, the wolves began to prowl closer and closer to the Culps' shack. At night their morose howls echoed eerily from the woods until the hunters' cabin fever became unbearable. With each new chorus of yelps, Bucky paced back and forth near the fireplace while his pa compulsively oiled his rifle.

One night Bucky swore the wolves' baying originated in the side yard. Sure enough, when he checked outside in the morning, he found four sets of fresh paw marks by the door. Luckily, the boy had hung the frozen deer carcass high above the ground because he had seen traces in the snow of the wolves' frantic leaps to try to reach it.

Now besides his loaded rifle, Bucky began to carry a razor sharp hatchet and a knife with a foot-long blade. Wolves normally holed up in burrows during the day, but with a scarcity of game fueling their hunger, the boy wasn't taking any chances. By the frequency of their sign, he could tell that a large pack had gathered in the hollow. And by the way they had encircled the cabin at night, it wasn't difficult to figure out who had become their prey. Even when Bucky went to fetch firewood from the stack in the backyard, he now went heavily armed.

Iroquois was even more worried about starving to death than he was about the wolves. He kept telling Bucky, "Once we run out of food, we can always boil our spare moccasins. They'll keep us going for awhile longer."

"If you say so, Pa," Bucky always agreed with a laugh. Then he would go out and set a few more snares.

By December, Iroquois' greatest fears were about to be realized. October's deer had been eaten long ago, and they had just finished the last of the potatoes. But on the very day that the moccasins were to be sacrificed, Bucky stumbled upon a lone doe browsing greedily on beech leaves some thirty yards distant. He eased his rifle to his shoulder, yanked back the hammer, and drew a steady bead on the deer's neck. At the moment he squeezed the trigger, the doe caught his scent and leaped straight into the air to free herself from a snowdrift. Bucky's bullet ripped through her gut, and off she bounded in panicked flight. There was no time to reload, so Bucky rushed the wounded animal. He ran down the doe from behind, leaped on her back, and began bashing wildly at the top of her head with his hatchet. Finally, the animal collapsed in a squirming heap. Bucky continued to hammer away until crimson brains leaked from her ears. Although he got kicked four or five times, he hung on until the deer's death throes ebbed away.

By the time he staggered to his feet, Bucky was covered with blood. He gutted the deer with a practiced hand and immediately began dragging it back to the cabin. He was far too worried about wolves to mind the throbbing bruises left on his legs by flailing hooves. Twilight came early in the winter, and Bucky was so intent upon getting home, he almost forgot to reload his rifle. The way his heart raced, it was a wonder he remembered to retrieve it from the snowbank it had fallen into during his wild ride.

Sometimes fear can be a positive thing. In Bucky's case, it replenished a strength sapped by two months of undernourishment. It so spurred him that he dragged the deer nonstop through two miles of three-foot drifts. He plowed ahead through the snow, leaving tufts of deer hair and a wide trail of blood. He never stopped chugging until he butted down the cabin door in his hurry to get the doe to safety.

Iroquois woke with a start from his pine bough bed in front of the hearth. The lack of food had taken such a toll on him that he seldom left the shack anymore. His skin had grown sickly pale, and he had let his scalp lock grow out into a full head of greasy, unkempt hair. When he realized Bucky had killed a deer, he crawled from his bear skin blanket and shouted, "Damn! Are we gonna eat tonight!"

Iroquois helped Bucky hang the doe in a tree and peel off its heavy hide. They lugged a hindquarter inside to slice into steaks. Then Bucky took in the liver. The rest of the deer they hoisted high out of harm's way. By the time they had finished their butchering and had reattached the door on its frame, drops of deer blood were everywhere around the cabin.

That night the wolves went crazy. Drunk on the smell of fresh blood, they snarled and spit and rammed against the side of the shack. They yipped and screeched like the hounds of hell, leaping repeatedly at the deer suspended in the tree. When all their efforts failed, they turned on a scrawny wolf and ripped him from eyeball to belly. All that was left of the wretched beast was some scattered bones and fur when the Culps peered cautiously out the front door in the morning.

"That's the way of nature, boy," Iroquois said. "The weak gets theirselves eaten. Remember that—always."

"I will, Pa."

At midday the wolves still skulked about the perimeter of the shack, but neither of the men ventured outside. After getting kicked by the thrashing doe, Bucky was too lame to stir from the fire. His pa was too gorged with deer liver to move much, either. Not that Pa now moved much, anyway.

Iroquois had become so sluggish that Bucky began to wonder if something wasn't wrong with him beyond hunger. Ever since his beating in Smethport, he just hadn't been the same. He missed easy shots at deer standing broadside. He often forgot to take his powder horn or skinning knife into the woods with him. He even lost his appetite for the hunt. That afternoon, as usual, he spent staring into the hearth fire, listening to the wind imitate the baying of wolves.

"What's you thinkin' about, Pa?" Bucky asked in a voice edged with concern.

"About your ma. Our life in town. How she sweated. Died."

"I don't remember her much. Only her eyes. What was she like, Pa?"

"She was a lady," choked Iroquois. "So beautiful. I gave up the woods for her. Worked at the mill."

"At the mill?"

"You was just a tad. I'd have done anything. If only she'd have lived."

"Why did we come here, Pa?"

"Returned to my old ways," replied Iroquois, his voice assuming its usual gruffness. "Once she was gone."

Bucky watched a single tear trickle the full length of Iroquois' face. Frightened by this sign of weakness, the boy stuttered, "D-D-Do you think the wolves will come b-back tonight?"

"Don't know. Don't care. Put another log on the fire, boy."

Iroquois wrapped himself in his bear skin blanket and closed his eyes. The wind had risen to gale force and buffeted the cabin until the door shook on its hinges and the fire flickered and almost went out. The wind's howling was inescapable and equally as frightening as the wolf attack of the night before.

Bucky arose the next morning with his nerves rattled by the all-night storm. He puttered about the cabin, cooking deer liver, thankful for the fresh supply of meat. With no need to venture into the forest, Bucky melted lead in a tin pot and cast bullets in a handmade mold. The rest of the day he spent sweeping the cabin and sharpening his knife and hatchet. Between each chore, he dozed restlessly at the table.

In the middle of the afternoon, Bucky woke from one of his naps to find himself alone. He was about to call out for his pa when a shriek echoed from the direction of the spring.

Bucky leaped for his rifle and bolted out the door. A fearsome snarling echoed from the spring as ten starving wolves tore into Iroquois. They had been concealed in the underbrush waiting for their chance, and when the man had gone to fetch a bucket of water, they surprised him. He hadn't even had time for a shot when they leaped from the laurel. He used his gun like a club until they bowled him over and buried him under a gray wave of bristling bodies.

Bucky came at them at a dead run, and his first shot tore through three of the wolves that squirmed on top of Iroquois. Two of the beasts died instantly, and the third retreated yelping into the brush. That left seven other flashing sets of fangs that tore mercilessly at the downed man. Bucky smashed another wolf's skull with his rifle butt and then drew his ax and began hacking at two others that whirled to face him. He severed the first one's snout with one blow, and the other he gored in the side. A fourth wolf leaped at Bucky from his right, but the boy dodged agilely and hacked off the beast's hind leg. Pa had quit struggling by then, but Bucky slathered and snarled and struck at the wolves with a renewed fury until he drove them from the field.

As Bucky grabbed Iroquois by the scruff of the neck and began dragging him wildly toward the cabin, two wolves came blasting back out of the brush. The boy crouched low and yanked his knife from its sheath. He jammed the blade deep into one leaping beast's ribs. The other hit him from the blind side. Bucky and the second wolf rolled back and forth across the yard without either able to get the advantage. The boy had his assailant by the throat and struggled desperately to keep its jaws from closing on his jugular. In the end, adrenalin and man strength won out. With one last powerful snap, Bucky broke the wolf's neck. While he rolled free from the dying beast's embrace, the first wolf leaped toward him only to collapse inches away with the knife protruding from its heaving chest.

Bucky withdrew his weapon and crawled to his father's side. It was already too late. Iroquois' rent throat was awash with black blood, and his eyes stared vacantly into the winter sky. Bucky closed his father's eyelids and dragged the body inside the cabin. He returned to the place of ambush and found four dead wolves piled up by the spring. Two others he had grievously wounded, and two more lay dead in the yard behind him.

It wasn't until after Bucky retrieved the Kentucky rifles that the tears began to flow. Then he moved listlessly toward the cabin, slammed the door shut, and slumped at the table in a daze. Hours passed before he became aware of the sound of sharp teeth gnawing on bone that echoed from the side yard. Only then did Bucky fully understand that Pa was gone.

Chapter Eight
A Call to Arms

Bucky washed the blood from his father's corpse and dressed it in a clean buckskin jacket decorated with dyed porcupine quills. He shaved off Iroquois' greasy hair until just a scalp lock remained. Then the boy sat cross-legged next to the body and chanted and moaned until night slipped away with the surviving wolves.

The next morning when Bucky found the ground was too frozen to give Pa a decent burial, he dragged his father's corpse to a neighboring beaver dam. There he wrapped it in a heavy logging chain and lowered it through a hole he chopped in the ice. At least, under water, Pa will be safe from wolves, he thought.

After Bucky submerged Iroquois' body, he wandered aimlessly around the frozen pond. The wind knifed from the bleak winter sky, but he did not feel its bite. He felt lonely and lost and a little afraid. But he also knew he would survive if he followed the lessons his father had taught him.

Bucky spent the rest of the winter mourning Pa. To ease his grief, he started a trap line and caught many fine beavers in the dams they had built in Potato Creek. It took him all morning to check his twenty-four traps. Each was made of heavy steel and had powerful spring-loaded jaws that were efficient in snaring the thick-bodied rodents. On the days the traps were full, Bucky skinned beavers until dark. Afterward, he collapsed on his pine bough bed, too exhausted to dream of ferocious, slashing fangs.

Since Bucky ate only one meal a day, the doe hanging in the tree lasted him until the end of January. Beaver meat was tough and greasy, but he ate that, too, with a relish only a starving man can appreciate. February brought a slight thaw, and Bucky killed another doe and snared several tasty grouse. In the forest Bucky strayed across an occasional clawed paw print of a wolf. The survivors of the pack that killed Iroquois no longer hunted near the cabin.

Spring finally broke in April. Bucky shouldered a bundle of furs and his pa's forty-five caliber rifle and headed for the annual Smethport rendezvous. Despite his meager diet, he had grown several inches during the difficult months and was now the height of his late father. He resembled Iroquois in other ways, too. Not only did he possess the same lanky build, but he also wore the Culp intensity on his gaunt, hawk-like face. Add to that a freshly shaved scalp lock, and not many who saw him would dare call him "boy" unless deliberately looking for trouble.

Bucky took his time covering the ten miles to town. He stopped often to munch wild leeks and to stare at the V's of returning geese that honked toward the north through the chilly, blue sky. Red-winged blackbirds shrilled in the willows, and a downy woodpecker punched its beak against a hollow tree. The forest floor was a colorful carpet of red and white trilliums. Bucky chuckled, remembering how Iroquois always called the flowers "stinkpots."

He emerged onto the East West Road around midday and went straight up the street toward the Jewetts. When Jimmy answered his familiar knock, Bucky hardly recognized his friend. Jimmy, too, had sprouted up over the winter. Gone were the baby fat and the paunch. He wore a pressed shirt that was cut to reveal broad shoulders and gangly arms. On his flat Scandinavian nose perched a pair of spectacles that seemed to bring an intensity to his eyes. The wavering whine still played in his voice, though, and his step remained clumsy and unsure.

"Hey, it's Bucky," Jimmy shouted as he gripped his friend's hand and practically dragged him in the door.

"Bucky, it's so nice to see you," chimed Mrs. Jewett, drying her hands on an oversized apron. "My, how you've sprung up."

As usual, Bucky blushed a bright crimson when Jimmy's ma hugged him. She looked prettier than ever with her dark hair framing a delicate, wan face. If his ma was even half that pretty, no wonder Iroquois loved her like he did.

"My father's off raising money for the new church he wants to build," said Jimmy.

"Yes, our congregation has really grown," added Mrs. Jewett proudly. "My husband has worked hard to spread the Lord's word here in Smethport. We had three new families join the church last week alone. There are no longer enough seats for everyone in the chapel. Maybe you and your father would like to come some Sunday."

Bucky's face went suddenly blank. He shifted his weight from one foot to another as his eyes traveled from Jimmy to Mrs. Jewett and back again. Finally, he mumbled in a subdued voice, "Pa is dead."

"You poor dear," gasped Jimmy's mother. "How on earth did it happen?"

"Wolves!"

Jimmy and Mrs. Jewett shuddered at the evil emphasis Bucky gave the word and then rushed forward to smother their friend in a heartfelt embrace. Bucky tried to tear away, but something deep inside him needed the touch of another human more than anything in the world.

"What are you going to do now?" asked Jimmy's mother tearfully.

"Hunt."

"But all alone in the woods?"

"Yes."

"Oh, Bucky," choked Mrs. Jewett, daubing at her eyes with a handkerchief. "Please come into the kitchen and have some lunch with us."

Jimmy's mother fetched her guest a plate from the cupboard and motioned for him to sit next to her son. She passed him a platter heaped with homemade bread and sliced cheese. Although Bucky hadn't eaten much in two days, he had a hard time choking down one sandwich after the Jewetts' outburst of emotion.

Jimmy had an equally difficult time eating, and after pushing away a half-full mug of milk, he said, "Why don't we take a walk downtown, Bucky? I've got something to show you."

"All right. Thanks for the meal, Mrs. Jewett."

"You're welcome here anytime, Bucky," replied Jimmy's mother as she gathered up the dirty dishes. "Be sure you boys are back in time for supper."

As soon as Bucky and Jimmy closed the front door, Jimmy squeezed his friend's shoulder and blurted, "Have you heard about the war yet?"

"War?"

"The Rebs fired on Fort Sumter and have seceded from the Union."

"What's that mean?"

"Why, it means that the Southerners have decided to form their own country," explained Jimmy, "because they want to keep using slaves on their cotton plantations."

"Why's that bad?"

"The planters are buying and selling black people like they would a horse or mule. My father says it's shameful to treat God's children like that. And my teacher says that President Lincoln considers the Rebels' secession as an outright attack on the Constitution. Take a look at this!"

Jimmy led his friend to the front entrance of the Bennett House where several handbills had been posted on the wall and pointed excitedly at the most prominent one of the lot. "Well, what do you think?"

"Think of what?" echoed Bucky, after staring blankly at the handbill.

"Oh, you must be farsighted. You can only see deer completely hidden in the brush. Here, let me read it to you:

VOLUNTEER RIFLES
MARKSMEN WANTED!

By Authority of Governor Curtin, a Company will be formed this week of Citizens of McKean and Elk Counties, who are prepared to take up arms immediately, to support the Constitution of the United States and defend the Commonwealth of Pennsylvania. I am authorized to accept at once for service, any man who will bring in with him to my head quarters a Rifle which he knows how to use.

Come forward Americans, who are not degenerate from the spirit of '76! Come forward in time to save the city of Washington from capture–in time to save the flag of the Union there from being humbled as it has been at Fort Sumter.

Smethport, April 17, 1861   Thomas L. Kane

Head quarters at the Bennett House, Smethport. Muster roll at the same place and questions answered. Apply without further notice."

It took Bucky a moment to digest all that he had heard. Then he said matter-of-factly, "I have a rifle and know how to use it. But I shoot animals. For food."

"With the way you handle a weapon, just think of how great a soldier you would be," bubbled Jimmy. "Wouldn't you like to protect your country and help Mr. Lincoln keep the

Constitution in one piece? Colonel Kane is in town right now, and I plan to sign up tomorrow to fight with him."

"But why do you wanna leave home? You have a good mother and father. You wear nice clothes. Have plenty to eat."

"I already told you. I want to fight the Rebels and make them quit using slaves."

"But you don't even like to fistfight. How are you gonna kill somebody?"

"I . . . I . . . I . . ."

"Come on, Jimmy. What's the real reason you wanna run away?"

Jimmy rolled up his shirt sleeves, revealing deep bruises that ran the length of both arms. "The kids at school," he finally muttered, "keep picking on me. When I come back from war a real hero, that'll show them I'm no sissy."

"But what'll your ma say?"

"I'm afraid to ask her."

"But won't she be hurt?"

"I don't care. I've got to show those bullies that I'm no mama's boy."

"If you was to go, why would you follow this Colonel Kane?"

"Shoot! He's only the most famous man in these parts. He's been a lawyer and a U.S. Commissioner. He was educated in Paris, France. His brother was an explorer who went to Greenland and parts of China. Talk about an exciting family! My mind's made up. I'm going with him."

Bucky shrugged his shoulders and made a face. "What if you go away an' gets killed? I already lost my pa . . . an' . . . an' you can't shoot. Maybe it's best that I do go."

"Oh, Bucky! Do you really mean it? We're going to have ourselves a real-life adventure!"

"An adventure? That's a funny way to describe shootin' other men."

"But we still do have one little problem, Bucky."

"What's that?"

"I heard that we have to be at least eighteen to sign up."

"Well, Jimmy, I ain't gonna lie about my age."

"The way I got it figured, you won't have to."

"Really?"

"Yeah, a guy I overheard said that all you gotta do is write the number eighteen on a piece of paper and put it in your moccasin."

"What good'll that do?"

"Then when the recruiting officer asks your age, you can truthfully say that you're *over* eighteen."

"But, Jimmy, ain't that like cheatin'? My pa always said to be honest with other men if you want 'em to respect ya."

"Ah, come on. Didn't you tell me how shrewd a trader your pa was? Was he always totally honest when he bartered with the rendezvous merchants?"

"But that was different. He was only tryin' to get the supplies we needed to live another year."

"Look, Bucky, there are lies, and there are untruths. An untruth *seems* right, but then again it isn't. You understand, don't you?"

"What I understand is a fella named Jimmy wants to go with Colonel Kane, and he'll do anything to get into the regiment."

"Yeah," Jimmy said. "That about sums it up, friend."

Chapter Nine

Birth of the Bucktails

The next morning Bucky and Jimmy slipped out of the house while Mrs. Jewett was hanging up washing in the backyard. With Jimmy leading the way, they hurried off down the street to join a group of lumbermen and hunters gathered outside the Bennett House. The majority of the crowd were rugged outdoorsmen dressed in red flannel shirts or buckskin. They were a bearded, robust lot used to living in the woods and surviving under the most arduous conditions. Like Bucky, they had fought like wildcats against blizzards, wolves, or anything else Mother Nature cared to serve up. Strong and fiercely free, they had come to take a crack at Johnny Reb.

The unruly crowd hadn't waited long before a diminutive officer dressed in a blue colonel's uniform emerged from the hotel's door. The officer had a bushy, black beard and black hair, and his dark eyes burned with patriotic fire. Although most of the woodsmen towered like trees over the colonel, they grew respectfully quiet when the jockey-sized man cleared his throat and barked in a deep voice, "Men, my name is Thomas L. Kane. I have come to Smethport to organize a rifle regiment and to lead it forthwith to Harrisburg. Captain Blanchard is waiting inside to sign up all interested patriots."

Colonel Kane held open the door, and there was a mad rush to see who could be first to sign the muster roll. The men jostled and shoved in the true spirit of frontier competition before rushing toward a jovial captain who was perched at the bar. "Step up, men, and make your mark," he invited with a broad grin. "What we need are men who can shoot. We don't care if you're good lookin' or smell like a summer rose."

The burly lumbermen and hunters guffawed and pushed forward to sign the roll. Captain Blanchard separated them into two groups. The men he didn't know, he told to wait by the door. To the men he recognized, he said, "I reckon you can shoot the eye out of a turkey buzzard. Go on over and see Surgeon Freeman. You shoot so good that he has to make sure you have a pulse! Yeah, the doc's gotta examine everyone of you boys. He'll probably hurt you more than the Rebs."

When Bucky was handed the quill pen, he stared dully at the captain until he was told, "Go ahead, sonny boy. Make your mark. You know, an X. Here. Like this. Then, you can go wait with the group over there by the hotel entrance."

"But I can shoot the eye out of a *flying* turkey buzzard," protested Bucky as he drew a set of crossed antlers on the roll.

"Well, that's what we're going to find out, sonny boy. Just as soon as everyone has signed."

Jimmy was next to step up to the bar. "Did they have a jailbreak over at the county school today?" asked Captain Blanchard after noting the boy's neatly pressed shirt. "You ain't gonna get many Latin lessons where we're going, laddie."

"I . . . I . . . I know," stammered Jimmy, blushing crimson.

"Oh, you do?"

"Yes, we're going to learn about the glories of war," he blurted as he signed with a flourish his full name, James Matthew Jewett.

"Ain't much glory found inside a pine box, laddie. Why don't you run along home to your mama?"

This last comment set off a barrage of rough laughter from the woodsmen waiting in line, and Colonel Kane strode inside the hotel to see what was causing the ruckus. With all the tall recruits gathered around him, the captain still hadn't seen his superior enter the room when he said, "By the looks of them fine clothes, James Matthew Jewett, you don't know a patch box from a rifle barrel. We ain't runnin' no finishing school. This here's the army. What do you expect to do in it if you can't hit a cow in the rear with a handful of sand?"

"W-W-Why, I've had lots of music lessons. I could be your drummer."

"Oh, sure you could," chuckled Blanchard. "How old are you anyway, laddie?"

"I'm over eighteen."

"Yeah in dog years!" howled a grizzled recruit.

"Or maybe he means eighteen months," suggested his buddy.

The captain was about to make another humorous observation at Jimmy's expense when Colonel Kane pushed through the crowd and snapped, "Blanchard, send the boy over to the surgeon. We can always use a spirited lad with an education."

Bucky gave Colonel Kane an approving smile. The man may be small in size, he thought, but he must be big in courage. I can follow a man who stands up against the pack.

Bucky was about to wave his congratulations to Jimmy when he felt a hostile stare boring into his back. Bucky turned to find himself face-to-face with the very same tangle-bearded giant that had laid a licking on his pa. The man snarled and glared at Bucky but did not leave his place in the enlistment line. Luckily, he was told to report to the surgeon, and before he could return, Bucky and his group were taken by Captain Blanchard to an impromptu shooting range set up behind the hotel.

The captain carried an armful of whiskey bottles which he set on a board one hundred paces from the firing line. Each recruit was given one chance to hit a predetermined bottle. He was not allowed to sit or lie down when his turn came. He had to shoot from the standing position. If he hit the target, he was sent on to Surgeon Freeman. If he missed, Blanchard told him, "Go home to Mama!"

Eight of the ten men who shot before Bucky shattered their bottles. A cheer went up from the spectators for each winner. The two that were unfortunate enough to miss slunk off to a chorus of hisses and catcalls. When Bucky stepped to the line, Captain Blanchard held up his hand and said, "So, Mr. Crossed Antlers, you think you can shoot the eye out of a flying turkey buzzard, eh? First, I think we ought to see if you can hit this!"

Blanchard took an acorn out of his pocket and held it up for the crowd's inspection. There was a gasp from the townsfolk as the captain paced off fifty giant steps and stuck the acorn in the crotch of a small sapling. Most of the spectators couldn't even see the target at that range, let alone imagine hitting it. Bucky waited for the captain to stand clear before he whipped his rifle to his shoulder, drew back the hammer, squeezed the trigger, and blew the nut into a spray of dust.

A roar went up from the crowd, and Captain Blanchard looked like he had just been served a plate of uncooked crow. "Get along to the surgeon," he grunted grudgingly. "Now it looks like my company's gonna have two kiddies to wet nurse."

Grinning broadly, Bucky wormed through the cheering crowd toward the front entrance of the Bennett House. He met Jimmy coming out the door, and they shook hands like they had each just won a twenty-five-pound gobbler at a turkey shoot. They were still congratulating each other when Captain Blanchard and Colonel Kane came strolling up the sidewalk deep in conversation.

"Overall, we got a pretty fine group of recruits," the colonel boomed with evident pride.

"Yes, sir," Blanchard agreed.

"You hear that, Bucky? A fine group of recruits," Jimmy whispered.

"A fine bunch, all right. Let's hope they don't ride you . . . us too hard," said Bucky.

"Don't worry about that. Colonel Kane will see us through."

"I gotta go see the doc now, Jimmy. You'd best hoof it home. Your ma will be worried."

"Okay, see you back at the house."

"And that young lad can surely shoot," continued the colonel as the boys went their separate ways.

"Culp. Yes, sir. Excellent shot. Has grit, too—for a half-breed."

"Just to be clear, Mr. Blanchard. All the men in this colonel's outfit are treated with the same respect. There are to be no exceptions. Do we understand each other, Mr. Blanchard?"

"Clear, sir. Very clear."

"This Culp. Does he have grit for two?"

"Two, sir?"

"That drummer boy. Does Culp have enough grit for him?"

"I suspect so, Colonel. They're like brothers. Something has them real close. I wouldn't worry about them holding up their end of things. That Culp has pride enough for both."

"I'm sure you will test them," Kane added thoughtfully.

"Only within bounds, sir."

"Don't break them, Blanchard. Men need their pride. Fact is, this outfit needs pride."

"Yes, sir!"

"Now, if we could only come up with an appropriate name for such a fine regiment of outdoorsmen. You know. A name that would be a rallying cry for these riflemen."

While they were speaking, the officers looked across the street and saw a deer hanging in front of a meat market. "Why not take a buck's tail?" Blanchard offered.

"That's just the thing!" Kane agreed and sent James Landrigan of his home village to cut off the deer's tail and model it in his hat for the rest of the men. Pretty soon the whole company was streaming across the street to hack off pieces of deer hide to use for insignias of their own.

Chapter Ten

MOTHER'S OBJECTIONS

"You're fit as a fiddle!" bellowed Surgeon Freeman when he finished examining Bucky. "Be back here at daybreak, young fella. You shouldn't have no trouble at all with the long march ahead of us."

Bucky grinned at the balding physician. Being examined was a new experience for him. He always doctored at home with Iroquois' remedies of roots and potions. But passing the physical didn't much surprise him. He slid his buckskin shirt over his head and pushed his way past the crowded bar where several sloshed woodsmen slapped him on the back and shouted, "Welcome to the regiment, boy. See you in the mornin'."

Although there was no sign of the hulking giant that had beaten Bucky's pa, several equally surly lumberjacks huddled near the hotel entrance. "I never thought I'd be goin' off to war with a stinkin' Injun," growled one towering woodcutter as Bucky slid past them.

"Me neither," agreed his partner. "If there was still a bounty on Injun scalps, that fella'd have hisself a little accident before he left town."

"An' how 'bout that drummer boy?" scoffed another bruiser. "How's that puny fella gonna fight Rebs? He ain't strong enough to help his mama with the washin'."

Outside the Bennett House Bucky darted down an alley and slipped off into the woods to retrieve his cached furs. Dark clouds scudded across the afternoon sky, and a bone-chilling wind rattled the leafless oak boughs. Several times Bucky swore he heard twigs snap behind him, and he thought about doubling back to see if he was being followed. Instead, he veered through a beech thicket, circled through some laurel, and headed straight for his concealed furs.

Bucky laid down his rifle and dropped to all fours to sweep the leaves and loose dirt from the door of his underground cache. While he unearthed his pack, the boy was engulfed by a shadow that loomed suddenly over him like a thunderhead. Bucky glanced over his shoulder to find himself cornered by the same tangle-bearded ruffian that had dogged him since their first encounter three springs ago.

"Now what's you got there?" roared the lumberjack.

"N-N-Nothing for you."

"Why, that looks jess like the pack of furs that somebody stoled from me yestiddy."

"N-N-No. Them's my pelts. I trapped them."

"Yer lyin'. You couldn't trap a rooster in a hen house. Gimme that pack, or I'll break yer neck."

When the musclebound lumberman bent to seize the furs, Bucky blinded him with a handful of loose dirt. The giant howled and stomped and groped wildly for the slippery boy who evaded him. Bucky snatched up his rifle and drove the butt end of the heavy stock into the huge man's stomach. A curse died on the lumberjack's lips, and he crashed to the earth like a felled hemlock. While the giant writhed grunting on the ground, Bucky grabbed his furs and fled into the brush.

Won't that fella ever quit hatin' me? wondered Bucky, weaving through a patch of scrub oak. Why, he's ornerier than a wildcat with a porcupine quill in his paw, an' twice as tough! Somehow I gotta whip him if I want any peace. Ain't gonna run . . . like Jimmy. Even if that black-bearded skunk does scare me.

Bucky headed straight for the merchants' booths after he stomped onto the East West Road lugging his heavy bundle. He had watched his pa barter with these men for years, so he copied his father's swagger when he approached a trader he knew to be honest in his dealings.

"Well, if it ain't Iroquois' lad," the man chuckled with a tug on his suspenders. "Where's the old man? Drinkin' his breakfast?"

"Pa's dead."

"I . . . I . . . I'm sorry, sonny. Didn't know. What can I do fer ya?"

"I joined the Bucktails, mister. I need some supplies."

"Well, you come to the right place. Let me take a look at them furs."

Bucky unwrapped the bundle and held up a huge beaver pelt. "What'll you give me for this?" he grunted.

"How 'bout a horn of gunpowder?" asked the merchant after twanging out a tune on his suspenders.

"You can keep that horn of powder, mister. But if you throws in two pigs of lead an' a bullet mold, I might consider it."

"Damn!" swore the trader. "It's like dealin' with Iroquois hisself. Okay. Okay."

"How about this dandy skin?" replied Bucky.

"I'll give you a wool blanket fer it . . . and this rucksack. They'll both come in mighty handy out on the trail."

"Okay!"

"It looks like you could use a new slouch hat, too, sonny. How 'bout this here black felt one? It's been real pop'lar with lots of other soldier fellas."

"I'll give ya these here pelts for it."

"It's a deal. I'll even pin a deerhide band on it fer ya."

Bucky still had several beaver plews left, and he said to the merchant, "Have any pistols, mister? I need to buy one for the drummer boy. He won't be carryin' no rifle. He'll need somethin' to protect hisself with."

"How 'bout this Colt army revolver? It fires six shots. Its forty-four caliber ball is mighty potent."

"No, I reckon that's too heavy for my friend. Got anything else?"

"Well, I got this here Smith & Wesson. It's nice and handy. Won't kick as much, either, bein' only a thirty-two caliber."

"How much?"

"Well, being you's goin' off to war an' all, I guess I'll take them last beaver skins, an' we'll call it even."

"No deal, mister, unless you throws in a box of cartridges."

"Oh, all right. You're jess like yer old man. An' that ain't bad!"

With a flattered grin, Bucky tried on his new hat and tilted the brim at a jaunty angle. Self-satisfied, he loaded the powder, lead, pistol, cartridges, and blanket into his rucksack and started up the street toward the Jewetts. When he came to the Bennett House, the boy noticed a large swarm of lumbermen gathered outside the entrance. The tangle-bearded giant was standing in their midst gesturing belligerently. He bellowed out his grievances to an audience that growled and grunted and agreed with his every word. Keeping to the opposite side of the street, Bucky hurried past with his hat pulled low over his eyes.

He sprinted the rest of the way to the Jewetts and cut around back to find Jimmy sitting on the porch swing.

"Where you been?" whispered his friend as Bucky set his rucksack and rifle near the back door. "Mother's been asking about you. It's almost suppertime."

"I've been gettin' some supplies for the trip. I got you somethin', too."

Jimmy had a hard time containing his enthusiasm when Bucky handed him the Smith & Wesson pistol. He didn't dare yell, or his mother would hear him. Instead, he hugged his friend until Bucky pushed him rudely away and hissed, "Come on. I'll show you how to shoot it."

"There's a gully over yonder," whispered Jimmy. "Let's go down there. Then we won't be late for supper."

"Won't your mother come out if we shoot that close to the house?" cautioned Bucky.

"No, she's scared to death of guns. Come on. She won't be able to see us, anyway."

Bucky set an uprooted stump against the gully bank and backed up fifteen steps. "All you gotta do to load your pistol," he instructed, "is push the latch, fold up the barrel, an' pop out the cylinder. Then, stick six cartridges in the cylinder an' put her back together. When you pull back the hammer, she's ready to fire."

"How do you know so much about revolvers, Bucky? I don't remember you or your father owning one."

"From a shooting contest at the spring rendezvous. The nice old fella that won the prize let me fire his Smith & Wesson. I didn't do no good with it, but at least I learned how it worked."

Bucky had Jimmy practice loading the pistol and showed him how to aim and shoot it. It was only accurate at very close range, and when Jimmy happened to blow splinters off the stump, he growled, "Take that, Johnny Reb!"

After they had shot up half a box of ammunition, Bucky said, "You're doin' real good, Jimmy. I think you should save the rest of the shells for all them bad Southerners you wanna kill."

"Ha! Ha!" said Jimmy, concealing the gun in his coat pocket. "We'd better go back now, anyway. Mother will be furious if we're not there to eat the chicken she's fixing for us. We have to keep her in a good mood tonight until we tell her we're leaving. I sure hope she understands."

"But what if she don't?" asked Bucky.

"She just has to. That's all."

The boys returned to the backyard as Mrs. Jewett bustled onto the porch. "Jimmy! Bucky!" she shouted. "Time to eat! Get in here this minute!"

After Jimmy's mother said grace, she loaded the boys' plates full of steaming chicken, roast potatoes, and thick slices of homemade bread. Jimmy sat playing with his food, but Bucky wolfed down his first helping before Mrs. Jewett even had time to return to her place at the table. "I declare, Bucky," she said, "I'm glad you didn't eat my silverware. Whatever you did today sure gave you a good appetite."

Jimmy choked a little while his mother served Bucky another helping. He poked at his chicken breast as if it were wormy and ate just the center out of the piece of bread. Finally, he cleared his throat and stammered, "M-M-Mother. I . . . I . . . I j-j-joined the army t-today."

"You did what? Oh, you're such a kidder, Jimmy."

"No, I'm serious. I j-joined the Bucktail Regiment. I'm going off to war . . . with Colonel Kane."

"Oh, Jimmy, you aren't old enough. More bread, Bucky?"

"Yes, I am! Colonel Kane himself said that he had 'a fine group of recruits.' He meant me, too, you know."

"But what will your father say? Couldn't you at least wait until he gets home before making your decision? He'll be back in a day or two from his fund-raising trip."

"Sorry, Mother. The regiment leaves at dawn tomorrow."

"But don't you need your parents' consent?"

"No, Mother!"

"Then how did you join?"

"All I had to do was sign the muster roll. The army doesn't think I'm a baby like you do."

"Watch your mouth, Jimmy! I have a mind to march right down to the Bennett House and have a talk with that Colonel Kane. Then we'll see who leaves in the morning."

"Mother, you wouldn't dare! I'm sick of you fighting my battles. That's why I have to go."

"Don't use that tone of voice with me, young man, or you can leave now!"

"That's fine with me!"

Mrs. Jewett jumped up from her seat, snatched Jimmy's plate, and threw it, food and all, into the slop bucket near the back door. "Get out!" she screamed. "If you think you know more than your mother, then you're not welcome under this roof!"

"Fine!"

Jimmy erupted from the table, knocking over his chair as he rushed for the kitchen door. He paused just long enough to snatch his jacket and hat off the coat rack before storming off into the twilight. Bucky rose to follow until Mrs. Jewett sobbed, "No, Bucky. Please! Don't go! I'm afraid to stay alone in this big house."

"But what will Jimmy think?"

"Right now I'm too hurt to care."

Bucky spent the night in Jimmy's bedroom listening to Mrs. Jewett's sobs echo through the wall. The distraught woman continued to weep until well past midnight when she finally fell into a fitful slumber. Even then she thrashed in her bed until Bucky was tempted to go wake her. When he thought of how Jimmy deliberately broke his mother's heart, Bucky wanted to hurt his friend in a more physical way.

As Bucky lay on the feather mattress, he wondered what possessed Jimmy to give up such a comfortable life. Without hunting, he had plenty of food. Without trapping, he wore rich clothes. Without logging, he lived in the finest home on the whole street. If I was in Jimmy's place, thought Bucky, I'd whip them bullies and learn about war in school.

Chapter Eleven

COMRADES AND ENEMIES

Bucky crawled out of bed before daybreak. He sat in a chair by the window until first light transformed vague shadows into maple trees. When he could see the houses across the street, he pulled on his buckskins and tiptoed down the stairs so he wouldn't wake Mrs. Jewett.

To Bucky's surprise, he found Jimmy's mother waiting for him in the sitting room. She was perched on the edge of the sofa with her head buried in her hands. She had on a worn housecoat and a nightcap and looked haggard from her restless night.

"Good morning, Bucky," she murmured as he crossed the room toward her. "Please excuse my appearance. I was too worried about Jimmy . . . to get dressed."

"You look fine, ma'am."

"Do you think my boy is all right? I'm so ashamed of how I lost my temper. I should have never thrown him out of the house like that. What was I thinking?"

Suddenly Mrs. Jewett burst into tears, sprung from the sofa, and threw her arms around Bucky's neck. The woodsman held her close, not knowing what to do or say. What he did know was that if she'd have been his own mother, he would not have put her through this agony.

"Oh, Bucky!" she sobbed. "Do you think you can talk to Jimmy for me? Get him to come home?"

"I can try, ma'am."

"He has to be hungry. Maybe now that he's had time to cool down, he'll give up the foolish notion of going to war."

"Maybe."

It took Mrs. Jewett several minutes to cry herself out. When she regained her composure she said, "Come into the kitchen, Bucky, and I'll fix you a nice breakfast. Are bacon and eggs okay?"

"I ain't never had 'em, but I'm sure I'll like anything you cook."

"Sit down at the table. I'm sorry to hold you up like this. I know you have to . . . report."

"Yes, ma'am."

"This Colonel Kane. What is he like?" asked Mrs. Jewett as she flipped strips of bacon in an iron skillet.

"He's a fair man. I already seen him stick up for Jimmy once. The colonel respects your son for his smarts. He said so in front of the whole company."

"Do you think Colonel Kane will be a good leader?"

"Yes, I do."

"Well, thank God for that. If my Jimmy has to leave me, it will be a comfort to know that he'll be serving under a fair, competent officer."

Mrs. Jewett scooped four eggs onto Bucky's plate, and he wolfed them with the same hunger he had displayed at supper. "I swear, Bucky Culp, you have a bottomless pit instead of a stomach," she clucked after watching the boy gobble half a pound of bacon and six pieces of bread.

"It's your cookin', ma'am, that makes me so powerful hungry. Everything you make is delicious."

"Well, you know you're welcome here anytime."

"I gotta go now, Mrs. Jewett. Thank you kindly for everything. I'll talk to Jimmy . . . if he'll let me."

Jimmy's mother gave Bucky a final hug when he stood up from the table. "Take care of yourself," she choked. "And promise me that you'll watch out for my son."

"I promise. Goodbye, ma'am."

Bucky fetched his rifle and rucksack from the back porch and headed down the street toward the drumbeats echoing from the center of town. Despite the early hour, the East West Road was lined with spectators. They waved and whooped at Bucky until the boy broke into a self-conscious trot.

The rest of the company had already gathered in front of the Bennett House, so Bucky ducked into formation where he saw the most buckskin jackets. The red-shirted lumberjacks formed a separate squad. They were all huge men with huge hangovers. They cussed and fumed while they waited for the officers to set the company in motion.

Finally, Captain Blanchard shouted, "Forward, men!" and the Bucktails proceeded up the East West Road to the waving of flags and the shrill of excited voices. The townsfolk cheered and howled and fired guns in the air until Bucky thought joining the regiment wasn't such a mistake. He cocked his hat over his eyes and stepped smartly to Jimmy's martial drumbeat. With all the hubbub, Bucky had no chance to convince Jimmy he should stay at home.

Jimmy marched behind the officers at the head of the column, flailing his drumsticks in a mechanical way. He stared straight ahead with his face frozen like a tin soldier. He did not acknowledge his mother when she tearfully hailed him from the boisterous crowd. Jimmy didn't trust himself to look at her. He felt guilty and angry and confused at the same time. But he also knew he had something to prove to himself when he heard his former classmates mimic Mrs. Jewett's plaintive calls of "Jimmy! My Boy! Jimmy!"

Colonel Kane was mounted on the back of his favorite horse, Old Glencoe. His pride swelled with the knowledge that these good provincial men knew their duty and took to discharge it. He led his McKean County Company southeast out of Smethport and saluted the crowd that lined both sides of the road well past the town limits. The colonel relished the glorious sunshine that glinted off his polished boots and saddle. His thoughts burned with patriotic zeal even after he was forced to dismount and lead his spirited, roan horse along the footpath that would take them up Potato Creek to its source some fifteen miles distant.

Fenton Ward had been appointed first lieutenant, and he ordered the soldiers to break rank and march by threes as the path narrowed in the forest. They tramped along for hours through a broad wooded valley surrounded by gently sloping hills. The walk was an easy one for the men hardened by the wilderness. To take their mind off their journey, they belted out "Yankee Doodle," "Pop Goes the Weasel," and their favorite drinking song, "Old Rosin the Beau."

Bucky marched with two good-natured woodsmen who introduced themselves as David Crossmire and Frank Crandall. David was eighteen and continually wore a big gap-toothed grin. Frank's reddish beard made him appear a little older than his twenty years. A hardy, good-natured laugh exploded from his throat at the least provocation.

Both men were lean, long-legged hunters who loved to brag about the big bucks they had killed. "You shoulda seed the twenty-point whitetail I shot last fall up Windfall Holler," David crowed after everyone had become acquainted.

"Sure it weren't an elk?" chuckled Frank.

"Nope! Biggest whitetail I ever bagged!"

"How far away was he when you shot?" asked Crandall.

"Why, had to be at least three hunnerd yards. Took him right through the neck runnin' full bore."

"Well, I'll be danged," snickered Frank. "We're gonna have to call you *Boone* Crossmire from now on."

Although Bucky was too shy to add much to the conversation, he felt at ease in the company of such men.

They, in turn, respected Bucky's quiet confidence. Having witnessed the shot he had made on Captain Blanchard's acorn, they were glad Bucky wasn't fighting for the Rebs.

The men marched until late afternoon, traveling nearly to the headwaters of Potato Creek. After they had made camp, Bucky and his new friends were sent out by Lieutenant Ward to see if they could shoot some fresh meat for supper. With Boone Crossmire leading the way, they crept along a brushy ridge, scanning the lower benches for game. They hadn't gone more than a quarter mile before Frank Crandall motioned toward the mouth of a laurel-infested hollow. There, not more than seventy-five yards below them, was a herd of doe feeding in an opening in the trees. The deer would have been easy targets if Boone's rifle hadn't misfired and sent the herd bolting for cover. Frank's shot went wide when the lead doe leaped at the thud of Boone's falling hammer, and only Bucky succeeded in bringing down his animal with a snap shot that downed the beast two steps before it disappeared into the brush.

"Hey," chortled Frank. "I thought hunters that killed twenty points always checked their percussion caps *before* going into the woods."

"Nice shot, Bucky!" shouted Boone to deflect Frank's insult. "Come on, let's see where you hit her."

Boone led the three hunters to where Bucky's deer lay collapsed in the laurel. Bucky's ball had passed through both eyes, killing it instantly.

"Good thing you didn't gut shoot her," said Frank. "We'da never been able to follow a blood trail through that nasty brush."

"After that shot, you oughta wear this in your hat," added Boone, cutting off the deer's tail and handing it to Bucky. "Get rid of that ratty strip of deer hide."

It was almost dark by the time the three hunters returned to camp, dragging the lone deer. It wouldn't feed a hundred men, but at least the officers and a few others would get their bellies full. Many of the soldiers were too drunk, anyway, to care about food. A hulking sergeant named Curtis had brought along three canteens of potent rum from Smethport. He served it up to his lumberjack cronies all evening and had just turned to offer a cup to Jimmy when Bucky came back to sit by the fire.

"Hey, sonny boy, have a little taste," he slurred. "Grow hair on your chest."

"No, Jimmy," warned Bucky, as his friend was about to oblige.

"Oh, go suck an egg!" menaced the drunk sergeant. "My buddy here's gonna drink with us men."

Jimmy shot Bucky a warning look and reached for the cup a second time. Before he could take it, Bucky slapped it from the huge sergeant's hand, and its contents spilled down Curtis' pant legs.

"Hey, that's a waste of good liquor, you gol-dang Injun whelp! I hate Injuns! Injuns killed my pappy an' grandpappy. Hey, ain't this Injun a friend of yours, Brewer?"

At the sound of his name, a tangle-bearded giant stepped from the shadows to glower at Bucky. "I owes ya fer chuckin' dirt in my eyes," he slurred. "Now I'm gonna rip yer head off!"

"You can try, you overgrown varmint. But I think you're too drunk to ketch me."

Brewer lunged at Bucky as he stood before the fire. Bucky dodged deftly, and the giant tumbled screaming into the licking flames. He rolled out the other side like a drunk black bear with his beard singed and his hair smoldering. He continued to roll until the fire in his beard and hair was extinguished and then reared up bellowing revenge.

A crowd of soldiers now formed a ring around the combatants. Brewer crouched low and began backing Bucky toward a group of his intoxicated buddies. As the drunk lumberjacks reached out to snare the boy, Boone and Frank pushed them aside, shouting, "No, you don't! This is between Bucky and Brewer!"

Distracted by the ruckus, Bucky glanced behind him just as the giant lashed out with a mammoth paw. The blow caught the boy square in the face, and he was dashed to the ground like a headshot buck. Brewer then leaped to crush his hated enemy beneath his full weight. Somehow Bucky rolled to the side, and the giant fell heavily on the ground, gasping for breath.

Bucky shook the cobwebs from his head and popped back to his feet, juking like a prizefighter. Using a tree for a crutch, Brewer pulled himself upright. He wheezed and swayed, while Sergeant Curtis howled, "Come on, Brewer. Kill him! Kill that gol-dang Injun whelp! Do you hear me? Kill him!"

Pricked by his friend's hatred, Brewer lowered his head and charged like a blood-crazed bear. Again, Bucky waited until the last possible moment before leaping aside while swinging a leg to trip the incensed giant. Instead of crushing the boy's ribs, Brewer tripped full bore into a hemlock trunk, knocking himself unconscious. As his big body slumped to the earth, Boone and Frank Crandall shook the dusk with their hearty, mocking laughter.

"That showed him," howled Boone. "That old boy ain't gonna bother nobody for awhile. I wouldn't want to wake up with his headache."

The men gathered around Bucky to slap him on the shoulder and make rude jests about the combat they had just witnessed.

"We oughta get them two to play David and Goliath at next year's Christmas play," chuckled one soldier.

"Yeah, if they don't kill each other first," cackled another.

Only Jimmy seemed miffed by the whole incident. When Bucky talked to him later in private, the drummer boy snarled,

"How could you embarrass me like that? I thought you were my friend."

"Embarrass you?"

"Yeah, I wanted to take a drink. You know. To fit in."

"Fit in?"

"You don't know how hard it is for me, Bucky. I can't shoot or fight like you, and the men treat me like I'm five years old."

"Do you think you can earn respect by gettin' drunk? Did the men respect the drunk who attacked me? Remember my pa? The night we found him outside the tavern? Do you wanna end up like that?"

"Oh, yeah? That'd never happen to me. I know I could hold my liquor. You sound just like my mother. I can't believe you sided with her like you did. Let me shiver all night alone in the street . . . while you snoozed comfortably in my bed."

"Jimmy, if I sided with your mother, I wouldn't be here now."

"Yeah, I almost believe that!"

"I jess stayed in the house 'cause your mother was scared to be alone with your pa away, an' all. You should be ashamed of how upset you made her. She bawled all night over you. I didn't get no rest."

Jimmy considered his friend's words for a moment and then burst into tears. Bucky put his arm around Jimmy's shoulder and talked quietly to him until he stopped sobbing.

Afterwards, Bucky rolled himself in his blanket but did not sleep. Why did Pa have to die? he wondered. I could be home now catchin' brook trout an' huntin' turkey. It's all that skunk Brewer's fault. If he hadn't beat the spirit out of my pa, he'da never been surprised by them wolves. He was too good a woodsman. Now all I got left is Jimmy. I gotta take care of him like I promised his ma. But what am I gonna do about Brewer? What am I gonna do? I reckon he ain't gonna quit 'til he gets me. Or dies tryin' . . .

As Bucky thrashed restlessly by the fire, his thoughts were interrupted by the subdued voices of Colonel Kane and Captain Blanchard murmuring from a neighboring campsite. "A lot of the men are asking where we're headed," said the captain in a guarded tone.

"I would have told them of our plans to rendezvous with the companies from Elk and Cameron Counties. I just didn't want them to get discouraged by how far they'll have to walk."

"Discouraged? These men? Nonsense, sir! Most of these hunters could walk two hundred miles and be just as fresh as if they took a Sunday stroll."

"Of course, you're right, Captain. I'll talk to the company tomorrow before we cross the divide to the Sinnemahoning River."

"By the way, sir, did you hear about the fight we had tonight while you were off scouting tomorrow's trail?"

"No."

"Well, Colonel, it started—"

Bucky broke into a sweat as the shifting wind scattered the captain's words like dry leaves. Only emphasized phrases like "drunken lout," "Culp dodged," and "need punished" fluttered from the muffled narrative.

Lumberjack reenactors arrive at the Bucktail encampment during the Bucktail reunion, August 19, 2000, at Ridgway, Pennsylvania.

Rich Adams, *right*, commander of Bucktail Regimental Association, discusses orders of the day with his officers. Rich maintains the regiment's Web site at http://www.pabucktail.com.

Bucktail reenactors, *left to right*, Jason Sunderland, 1st Pennsylvania Rifles, Company K; Ben Miller, 149th Pennsylvania, Company H; and Chris Shope, 1st Pennsylvania Rifles, Company B, snap to attention during the Bucktail reunion.

Bucktail lads relax after close-order drills.

Chapter Twelve

THE RATTLERS' DEN

Lieutenant Ward routed the soldiers out of their blankets well before the sun's rays jabbed over the horizon. As they moved listlessly about refueling their campfires, Colonel Kane emerged from his tent and called for their full attention. He competed with a hoot owl when he cleared his throat and began, "Men, many of you have been asking the officers where we are bound. By this afternoon, we'll be entering the Sinnemahoning River Valley to meet up with more members of our regiment at Driftwood. If the railroad tracks have not reached there yet, we'll be forced to build rafts and float downriver to Lock Haven to catch the train to Harrisburg. At the state capital we'll be sworn into the Army of Pennsylvania and receive our combat orders. Any questions?"

The men received the news in silence. They were still too sleepy to worry about the particulars of Colonel Kane's itinerary. Some stared transfixedly into their campfires, while others hopped from one foot to the other to get the circulation working in their legs.

"If not," Colonel Kane continued, "it has come to my attention that a fight broke out in camp last night during my absence. Men, I will not tolerate such rowdy behavior. We soon will have all we can handle fighting the Rebels. You need to conserve your strength for our battles with the enemy. From this moment forward there will be no more drinking of strong liquor allowed in camp. Anyone who fights or gets drunk will be severely reprimanded! That's all, men."

Bucky breathed a sigh of relief when the colonel disappeared back inside his tent. After eavesdropping on Kane and Captain Blanchard, Bucky had spent most of the night recalling harsh stories of other men's punishment for breaking army rules. He had jerked awake a dozen times from troubled dreams filled with firing squads, whip cracks, and the sting of repeated lashes. Whips reminded Bucky of uncoiling rattlesnakes, and he shivered when his mind made the association.

"Culp."

Bucky woke from his reverie to find himself facing Lieutenant Ward. "Yes, sir," he answered uneasily.

"Colonel wants to see you—immediately!"

"Y-Y-Yes, sir."

Bucky's pulse raced as he crossed the camp and was admitted into the colonel's tent by a corporal standing guard outside. "Y-Y-You wanted to s-s-ee me, sir," Bucky stammered when the bushy bearded Kane looked up from his breakfast.

"What's this I hear about you and Brewer?" the colonel asked, fixing Bucky with his fiery, dark eyes.

"N-N-Nothing, sir."

"Nothing? Then how did your face get so badly bruised?"

"Sorry, Colonel. I was just . . . defendin' myself."

"The way I heard it, you were defending the drummer boy. Loyalty to our friends is commendable, son, but not at the expense of the regiment. If all of you are fighting amongst yourselves, I doubt if you'll stand together when we finally face the Rebels. I had to call you in here to let the men know that brawling will not be tolerated. Is that understood?"

"Yes, Colonel Kane."

"Good! I don't want to have to talk to you again."

"No, sir. Thank you, sir."

A relieved Bucky saluted and ducked back out through the tent flaps. Waiting outside was the sullen-looking Brewer.

Bucky could hear the colonel's voice rise angrily when the giant stepped inside. "You really ought to be proud of yourself for picking on someone half your size!" growled Kane sarcastically. "Did it make you feel like a big man?"

Bucky was out of earshot before he could hear Brewer's reply. What he did notice, though, were Curtis' menacing glares of pure hatred. The sergeant was huddled with his lumberjack cronies around a neighboring fire, and his dark eyes smoldered as he snarled to those crouched next to him, "I'm gonna get that gol-dang Injun no matter what it takes. Them Iroquois butchered both my pap and my grandpa. Ever seed a man with his scalp hacked clean off? Ain't a purdy sight. Lots of blood!"

Curtis let his cronies ponder the image for a few seconds before thundering, "An' now that filthy half-breed got liquor banned from camp. Why, life ain't worth a pinch of sour owl manure if a man can't wet his whistle after he's done stomped the woods all day. No sir-ee!"

The sergeant continued to grumble while the company extinguished its fires, broke camp, and renewed its march up the gently rising trail. His giant friend, Brewer, stumbled along like a stunned ox beside him. Hung over and hurting, all the fight had drained out of him. Brewer's forehead was so swollen, it looked like he had been stung by a disturbed nest of hornets. His ears still burned from Colonel Kane's tongue-lashing, as well, and he pretended to ignore Sergeant Curtis' unrelenting outpourings of hatred.

After the Bucktails had hiked for two hours, Colonel Kane stopped at a spring along the trail to water Old Glencoe. The men welcomed the break, and those who had canteens filled them. Bucky, too, was hot and thirsty and immersed his whole head in the ice cold water. As he shook his dripping scalp lock, he rose to find himself hemmed in by Curtis and the hulking Brewer.

"Whatcha tryin' to do, ya stinkin' Injun, befoul the gol-dang spring?" barked Curtis. "It's bad enough we had to drink after a horse!"

Instead of getting into a shouting match with the sergeant, Bucky turned to Brewer and said, "A-A-Are you feelin' any better? W-W-Why don't we stop this feud now before someb'dy really gets hurt? I beat up your boy. You beat up my pa. Don't that make us even? If we fight again, we ain't gonna get off with just a warnin'. Colonel Kane will make a real example of us."

Brewer glared at Bucky with his red pig eyes as Curtis launched into another tirade. "Get away from us," he snarled, after bouncing Bucky off a rough-barked elm. "You've got a lot of nerve talkin' to my friend like that after you almost kilt him. 'Course, you ain't even!"

Bucky shot Curtis a wounded look and rubbed his scraped shoulder. He said, "I'm goin'. I ain't lookin' for no trouble. I guess nothin' I say is gonna make it right between us."

Curtis continued to cuss Bucky under his breath for the next five miles as the Bucktails passed through a dense hemlock forest that remained murky even on this bright spring morning. It was only after the regiment had made its passage over the divide between Potato Creek and the Sinnemahoning River that he took interest in the landscape. "Look at the size of them rocks," Curtis cackled, favoring the silent Brewer with a wicked wink. "I remember there bein' lots of caves up yonder. I wonder if that gol-dang Injun and his sissy friend would enjoy a little nature hike?"

The terrain changed drastically when the soldiers dropped over the ridge and started down the trail leading to the village of Emporium. The footpath followed a freestone stream that plunged wildly from one rocky pool to the next. Cabin-sized boulders choked with laurel hemmed them in on the other side in their rapid descent. The pebble-strewn path was treacherous, and the soldiers slid, skated, and fell often before reaching the valley floor.

Many of the former lumberjacks were now beginning to show the effects of the forced march. The muscular, big-torsoed loggers puffed and sweated and limped and cursed until Colonel Kane thought it best to make camp by early afternoon. That was okay by Jimmy, too. His bulky snare drum hung from an over-the-shoulder strap that had cut off the circulation to the boy's left arm. His legs were bruised from his numerous tumbles down the slope, and his army vocabulary had expanded to include epithets completely foreign to his strict Christian upbringing.

The company halted in a glen alive with tender leeks that the soldiers gobbled until their bellies burned and their breaths reeked. Fiddleheads were equally plentiful, and skunk cabbage bloomed in marshy spots next to the creek. The maples had just begun to turn crimson with sprouting buds.

Blue jays squawked their displeasure as the men gouged their imprint into the pristine meadow. They uprooted rocks for fire pits and dug trenches for foul latrines. Bucky and Jimmy were busy erecting the colonel's tent when Sergeant Curtis drew them aside and said with a shifty smile, "After you fellows get done, I got another chore for you."

"Yes, sir," said Jimmy, while Bucky merely grunted. There was something about the sergeant's eyes that reminded him of a reptile.

Half an hour later, Bucky and Jimmy reported to Curtis. The sergeant was unusually pleasant, and he grinned disarmingly when the two young soldiers approached his fire. "Well, men," he said. "I have worked up an awful hankerin' for rattlesnake meat. I would like you two to fetch me some."

Jimmy jumped at the word "rattlesnake" while Bucky said flatly, "How's we supposed to do that, sergeant? Ain't snakes still hibernatin'?"

"Yep."

"Well, how's we supposed to kill 'em if they ain't out sunnin' themselves?"

"That do kinda put you in a tight spot," chortled Curtis. "It looks like you'll jess have to go into their dens after 'em."

"But won't we get bit?" asked Jimmy, blanching.

"Could be."

"Even if we was to do what you ask, where would we find their dens?"

"Why, they're all around you, sonny boy," chuckled the sergeant, glancing up at the rocky hills that towered above the meadow. "I had a crew loggin' these parts a few years ago, and I know for a fact if you boys jess foller that ravine over yonder, you'll come to a nice big cave chocked-full of 'em."

"What if we won't do it?" spit Bucky.

"Well, then I'll have you and your friend brought up on charges of in-sub-or-di-nation."

Again, Jimmy jumped straight into the air. "I . . . I think we had better do what he says, Bucky," he squeaked after a moment. "Un-Unless you want to get sent home."

Bucky glared at Curtis before leading his friend back to their campsite to fetch his hunting bag and to fashion a crude torch from a pitch-dipped pine stick. This done, he and Jimmy began their ascent of the rugged ravine, which was much steeper than it first appeared. Much of their climb was straight up over moss-slick shale. Several times they nearly plunged to their deaths. Only Bucky's strength and some laurel brush handholds kept them from sliding off the cliff.

Both boys glistened with sweat by the time they hoisted themselves to the top of the ravine. Near the summit, the rocks were honeycombed with crevasses and small caves that made perfect cover for hibernating rattlers. Only one of these, though, was large enough for a man to enter. The opening in the rock was a yard high and four yards wide, and Bucky told his friend, "Stay here," before slipping inside with his lighted torch.

Bucky sprouted goose bumps as he crawled on his belly through the dank cave. A musty stench grew stronger in his nostrils the deeper he slithered into the lair. The torch sputtered and smoked until he could discern little ahead of him.

The boy squirmed forward some thirty feet and suddenly found his face inches from a mass of sleeping snakes. A large one's deadly head was pointing at Bucky's nose. When he struggled to back up, its forked tongue flicked wickedly from its mouth. Bucky's hand shot forward and nabbed the rattler behind the head. The wakening reptile sprung instantly to life, buffeting its mates with its writhing, three-foot length. In the ensuing struggle, the torch shook free from his other hand. It rolled across the damp cave floor until extinguishing itself in a shower of dying sparks.

Suppressing a scream, Bucky squeezed the snake in his right hand until it quit thrashing. Even then, he dared not release his grip. Not only did he need the meat for Sergeant Curtis, but if he let the snake go, it still might strike him. At the Smethport rendezvous he had seen lots of dead rattlers jab their fangs by reflex action.

Buzzing now came from every corner of the cave, and Bucky fought to remain calm. Carefully, he began inching backward out of the rattlers' den, knowing that a mad scramble would get him bitten. He continued to back toward the light behind him until he felt a snake slide against his left calf. He froze, sweating until it had slithered over him, and afterward continued even more deliberately than before. He was within five feet of the light when a warning buzz froze him again. An even bigger rattler than the one he gripped in his hand was coiled up directly behind him, blocking his escape. A pistol shot rang out, and the snake's poised head was blown into jam. The ricocheting bullet sung past Bucky's ear as he leaped backward to evade another rattler that struck at him from the darkness. Jimmy was there to catch his friend as he tumbled from danger into the light.

"Oh, thank God, you're okay!" wheezed Jimmy, helping Bucky to his feet. "I was scared to death I might have hit you instead of the snake."

"You did the right thing," gulped Bucky, evidently flustered. "Once I had to take a risky shot to save my pa."

"I knew you bought me this pistol for some reason," replied Jimmy. "It looks like all the practicing we did behind the house paid off, after all."

"I wish I'd had your gun when I come across this rascal," said Bucky, holding up the three-foot rattler he still held in a death grip. "What do you say we take this snake and feed it to Sergeant Curtis?"

"Amen!" agreed Jimmy with a broad grin.

Bucky carefully pinned the snake's head beneath a rock and cut it free from the long, scaly body with one emphatic slash of his knife. As the late afternoon shadows engulfed the ravine, he and Jimmy began their slow descent back to camp.

Nightfall fell on the Bucktails like the shadow of a swooping hawk. Sergeant Curtis, Brewer, and several other burly lumbermen gathered around a roaring fire to cuss and joke and gloat. "I'll bet them whiny, little kids is halfway home by now," howled Brewer.

"Yeah, you shoulda seed gol-dang Jewett when I told him to go fetch me a rattler," snickered Curtis. "His eyes popped out of his head like hardboiled eggs!"

"Yeah, that's the last we seed of them," agreed another logger, who munched on a chaw of tobacco. He pursed his lips to spit into the fire when a rattlesnake buzzed not two feet behind him.

The men scrambled for their guns and fired wildly in the direction the snake had just rattled. In an instant they were surrounded by half the company who came running to see what all the commotion was about. Sergeant Curtis reloaded his rifle and moved cautiously into the brush behind where his friend had been seated. When he reemerged, he was holding a decapitated three-foot rattler which was blasted full of holes. With the light from the campfire falling on the riddled snake, Jimmy and Bucky stepped smirking from the shadows.

"Hey, Sergeant, I see you found the rattler we caught for you," said Bucky innocently.

"Shouldn't be too hard to cook, either," added Jimmy. "Now that you've got him gutted."

Sergeant Curtis' reply was lost in the howl of laughter that spilled from the gathered company. He was about to pitch the snake into the bushes when Colonel Kane appeared at their fire and commanded, "I'll take that, Sergeant! Why don't you come along to my tent and explain to me how a hibernating rattlesnake just happened to make its way into our camp."

Chapter Thirteen

Drunk in a Pig's Ear

The Bucktails marched into Emporium late the next day. The soldiers were drenched from a steady downpour that had fallen for several hours, and their limping, sodden forms looked like specters emerging onto Main Street from a veil of fog. Even Colonel Kane now walked, his horse having thrown a shoe while navigating the rocky divide. The rain ran from his drenched hat and down his neck, and he ordered the column to halt in a sea of mud that once was the town square.

"Men," commanded the colonel, trying to control a cough that racked his frail frame, "we're going to spend the night here in Emporium. The officers will be staying at the hotel just up the street. Enjoy your liberty. It'll be the last time you'll have any until we reach Harrisburg. We'll meet back here at dawn. Fall out!"

Thus dismissed from the ranks, Sergeant Curtis gave a whoop and led his squad on an assault of the nearest tavern. The tavern was marked as such by the sign of a pig's ear that hung over a set of swinging doors. Curtis' squad looked like stampeding cattle to the bemused townsfolk that had gathered to gawk at the regiment. No one would have guessed by the swiftness of their charge that the sergeant's soldiers had just stomped over fifteen miles of difficult terrain. Soon the men's weariness and soreness of foot would be forgotten in the bottom of a brown jug.

Boone and Frank weren't drinking men. They joined Bucky and Jimmy to amble along the mud streets and stare at the boarding houses, hotels, and three newspaper offices. They wandered until almost dark down by the swollen Sinnemahoning River where a grist mill and a lumber mill hummed with activity.

After a dinner of cheese, bread, and coffee, the soldiers loafed outside a blacksmith's shop, watching the smithy make shoes for Colonel Kane's horse, Old Glencoe. The powerful man hammered a piece of hot metal into a U on his anvil and sized it for the patient beast. Meanwhile, a covey of local girls in homemade dresses and turban hats gathered across the street. The girls glanced coyly at the Bucktails. They giggled, gawked, and preened to draw attention to themselves.

"By the way them gals is watch' us, you'd think we're gen-uine war heroes," chuckled Boone.

"They's real purty, though, ain't they?" said Frank.

"I'll say!" gushed Jimmy.

"They sure beat the females back in Smethport," grinned Boone.

"Why's that?" asked Jimmy.

"Because at least these gals don't bark or howl."

"What do you think of them, Bucky?"

"They don't interest me much."

"Why not?" joshed Boone. "Because they don't know how to skin a deer or chew its hide to make soft leather?"

"I don't want no Indian wife," said Bucky.

"Oh, yeah?" said Jimmy. "Then what kind of woman do you want?"

"Someday I'll live in town and work at the mill like my pa used to. The woods are too lonely. When I marry, I'll choose a fine lady . . . like your mother."

"My mother!"

"Yes, someone I can respect."

"I don't believe you said that, Bucky! My mother! No wonder you stayed with her our last night in Smethport!"

"What do you mean by that, Jimmy?"

"Hey, me an' Boone are gonna chat them gals up," interrupted Frank. "If you two are done with your squabble, you're welcome to come along."

Boone and Frank strutted across the street and bowed in an exaggerated way to the tittering town girls. Their giggles intensified when the soldiers complimented them on their hair, dresses, hats, and vanilla perfume.

Jimmy, meanwhile, continued to glare at Bucky and said, "I think I need a good stiff drink of whiskey."

"But what would your mother say?"

"What's the difference? She already kicked me out of the house."

"Don't you think you'd be better off writin' her a letter of apology than goin' to the tavern?"

"*Me* apologize?"

"If you were a man, you—"

"I'll show you how much of a man I am," bawled Jimmy. "I'm going to outdrink Curtis' whole squad. And you can't stop me."

Before Bucky could dissuade him, Jimmy turned heel, sprinted across the mud street, and disappeared through the swinging doors of the Pig's Ear. Bucky could hear a howl of surprise when his friend entered the tavern followed by chants of "Jewett! Jewett! Jewett!"

Jimmy was the center of attention as soldiers and town drunks alike leered at him from the crude wooden benches and bar stools. Sergeant Curtis cleared a space at his table, and, with a feigned wave of friendship, invited Jimmy to take a seat. Jimmy's money was no good, either, as the soused soldiers bought him round after round of white lightning. It wasn't long before the boy was dancing the jig with big Brewer and chugging pints of rum with a local lush.

"Where's you boys headed?" slurred the lush after wiping his mouth on his raveled shirt sleeve.

"We's gonna raft down the Sinnemahoning," boasted Brewer. "Startin' at Driftwood."

"Yous better be careful," warned the lush.

"Why's that?" burped Jimmy.

"'Cause there's dang'rous rapids. And big pumas that eats men for breakfast."

"I ain't afraid of nothin'!" scoffed Brewer. "Bring 'em on!"

"Yeah," echoed Jimmy. "Bring 'em on! Me an' Brew-er can handle anything!"

Bucky paced back and forth outside the Pig's Ear, listening to the intoxicated howls of the men inside. When Jimmy's squeaky voice rose above the other revelers, Bucky clenched his fists in rage. Why do I bother wet-nursin' that weasel? he thought. After the crack he made about me an' his ma, I shoulda thumped him. An' how can he go get drunk after I fought Brewer to keep him out of the rum? My life woulda been a lot simpler if I'da jess gone back to the hollow. No wonder Pa liked it out there so much. Weren't no men to cause him trouble. Seems like that's all I've had since I run across Jimmy!

Finally, Bucky shook his head and stomped angrily back up the street toward Boone and Frank, who again lounged in front of the blacksmith shop. "How did you fellas make out with them gals?" he asked after he'd had time to cool down.

"We made 'em giggle a lot," winked Boone.

"They had more feathers in their heads than they had sewed on them turban hats," added Frank. "They was too young to leave their mamas."

"What became of Jimmy?" asked Boone. "Is he off poutin' somewhere?"

"He stomped off to the tavern," growled Bucky.

"Why, he'll get hisself killed!"

"I tried to stop him."

"Hey, where are we gonna sleep tonight?" asked Frank. "We don't have no money like old Jimmy."

"I'll bet he don't have none either by mornin'," chuckled Boone.

The blacksmith had just finished putting away his tools when he said, "I'd be proud if you slept here, boys. There's some nice soft hay over yonder in my stable. Ain't fancy, but at least you'll stay dry."

"Thanks, mister." said Boone. "I reckon we'll take you up on that. We'll even return the colonel's horse for you in the mornin'."

Bucky left his rifle and rucksack with his friends and excused himself.

"Where're you going?" laughed Frank. "Out to water the lilacs?"

"No," chortled Boone. "I'll bet he's goin' to get smashed with his old buddy, Jimmy."

Bucky waved disgustedly and ambled off alone down the dark street, fighting the urge to drag Jimmy out of the tavern and give him a tongue-lashing he wouldn't soon forget. But if he embarrassed Jimmy again in front of Curtis and the others, he would risk losing his friendship forever. However, if he didn't interfere, he would be breaking his promise to Mrs. Jewett. His thoughts were further jumbled by the bellowed strains of a popular drinking song that echoed from the bowels of the Pig's Ear:

When one's drunk, not a girl but looks pretty.
The country's as gay as the city.
And all that one says is so witty.
A blessing on brandy and beer!

Bring the cup! Fill it up! Take a sup! Take a sup!
And let not the flincher come near!
And let not the flincher come near!

Oh, give me but plenty of liquor.
I'd laugh at the squire and vicar.
And if I'd a wife, why, I'd kick her
If e'er she pretended to sneer—

The song came to an abrupt end with the shattering of glass and the crash of overturning furniture. As Bucky stared through the gloom, he saw the swinging doors of the tavern burst open and a giant bartender emerge gripping Sergeant Curtis by the scruff of the neck and the seat of the trousers. The bouncer gave his charge the bum's rush into a puddle of cold slop that had coagulated in the street like a pig wallow. Curtis skidded on his face and struggled to regain his feet like an upended mud turtle. Before he could right himself, Brewer and two other soldiers came crashing down on top of him. As Bucky watched them squirm and curse and howl, he shuddered uneasily and ducked inside the Pig's Ear to rescue Jimmy.

Jimmy lay passed out on the sawdust floor, and two drunks were rifling through his pockets when Bucky rushed into the room. Bucky leaped forward to collar the rascals, only to find himself staring at the wrong end of the same pistol he had given his friend back in Smethport. While Bucky watched helplessly, the drunks snarled, sidled around a table, and bolted out into the dark street.

Bucky bent over his friend, whispering, "Jimmy! Jimmy!" When the boy still did not respond to a sharp slap in the face, Bucky shouted, "Bartender! A glass of water!"

The bartender was the size of a hogshead, and his muscles bulged beneath his shirt. Nonchalantly, he poured himself a tankard of ale. Then he took a long drag on his cigar and said with a sneer, "There's plenty of that over yonder in the river, sonny boy. Here we only serve liquor."

Choking back an angry reply, Bucky watched the hulking man produce a billy club from under the bar. Sensing the bruiser's ill intent, he grabbed Jimmy under the armpits and dragged him backwards across the floor and out into the cool night air. Brewer and Curtis groaned softly from where they'd been deposited in the muddy street. Bucky pulled his friend past them to the safety of the blacksmith's stable.

"Boy, you're gonna be in great shape to march tomorrow," Bucky grunted to the unconscious Jimmy. "Now how much like a man do you feel?"

Chapter Fourteen

The Thunderstorm

Dawn came much too early for Sergeant Curtis and his hung-over cronies. The rest of the company was already in formation, when pale and muddy, they staggered half-dead down Main Street. By far, Brewer looked the worst of the lot. Both of his eyes were blackened from his encounter with the Pig's Ear bartender, and his beard was caked with dried vomit. Curtis, though, looked pretty rough himself. His hair stuck out from under his hat like a rat's nest, and he limped like a lame horse being led off to the glue factory. He growled deeply in his throat when Boone and Frank made piggie noises as he took his place in the ranks.

Jimmy didn't even know where he was when Bucky, Boone, and Frank took turns leading him down the street minutes before Curtis' crew made their appearance. Jimmy's eyes wouldn't focus, and his head pounded like the inside of a hammered drum. His face was so white that Boone said, "I've seed day-old corpses with more color."

As the Bucktails tramped out of Emporium, the sun broke free from the retreating clouds. The company followed a narrow Indian path that snaked along the Sinnemahoning River. The trail wound and dipped and rose and dipped again until the dancing partners, Brewer and Jimmy, looked ready to pass out. Colonel Kane, though, never slackened the brisk pace, and Boone began to take bets on which of the drunks would be the first to fall out of the ranks. Somehow, neither did. Although Brewer and Jimmy stumbled along like zombies exhumed from a grave, their legs just kept churning.

Below Emporium, the terrain was more rugged than anything Bucky had ever seen. When the valley narrowed, the hills were replaced by roundtop mountains choked with hemlocks. In some places sheer shale cliffs rose hundreds of feet above the trail to remind Bucky of his encounter with the den of timber rattlers. Adding to his uneasiness were the pale, peeling sycamores that bordered the river banks. These trees glowed like transplanted ghosts reaching to snare him with their scaly, skeletal limbs.

While Bucky gawked at the foreboding landscape, Boone, who marched beside him, said, "Kind of scary, ain't it?"

"What do you mean?"

"The way the mountains hem us in."

"Yeah!"

"Did you ever notice how red them hills look this time of year?"

"It's the buds comin' on the trees."

"To me," said Boone, "it's like the hills are bleedin' from every pore."

"I don't like this valley much, either," admitted Bucky. "The place looks like it leads straight to hell."

"No," cackled Boone. "Hell was back there in Emporium. Just ask Brewer or Jimmy."

Gradually, black clouds swallowed up the sun, and thunder ricocheted off the mountains. "Hell of a place to get caught in a storm," Bucky heard Colonel Kane mutter to the captain.

They were traveling the narrowest part of the trail where it cut around a cliff. A wall of stones rose above them, and another plummeted into the river below. As a precaution, Colonel Kane dismounted from Old Glencoe and led the suddenly skittish animal on foot.

The sky continued to darken, and the wind howled until the sweating men shivered in their shirts. When the rain finally came, it beat unmercifully on the company, making the footing slick and the men nervous. For the next hour the lightning flashed ominously around them until all feared for their lives.

Although their progress had slowed to a crawl, Brewer and Jimmy looked even more zombielike than before. Brewer was having an especially difficult time keeping his feet. Twice he almost slid off the edge of the cliff. Finally, Bucky and Boone held up the giant between them and skidded him along the path like a hairy log. Frank latched on to Jimmy just to be on the safe side.

"Hey, Brewer," grunted Boone after they had struggled several hundred yards along the slippery path. "You're the one guy who should be thankful for this rain."

"Why's that?" asked Bucky, mimicking the giant's voice.

"Because now you smell a lot better."

Although Brewer was hurting too badly to answer, Bucky and Boone knew he was not pleased by his piglike stare.

The Bucktails slopped along for another two miles before the path widened and the thunderstorm moved east down the valley. There was still no place to stop and build a fire, but at least now they were out of danger. Brewer started to show signs of consciousness now, too. Finally, he shook his giant head, stood on his feet, and pushed away the two men who had carried him as if they were made of straw.

"I owe you two," he seethed through clenched teeth. "You make Brewer look like he can't pull his own weight. You watch. I'll get you!"

Bucky and Boone couldn't believe their ears. Here they had just saved Brewer's bacon, and now he was threatening to pummel them.

"Hey," said Boone, staring coldly at his antagonist. "Do you know what Colonel Kane woulda done to you if you'd fallen out of rank? Don't you know the trouble you'd be in?"

"It don't matter. I'll get you. You an' that Injun."

Brewer tottered up the trail and rejoined his lumberjack friends. Bucky just shook his head and then said to Frank, "How's Jimmy doin'?"

The drummer boy moaned a little at the sound of his name, and his eyes fluttered and popped open. "Where am I?" he echoed and stared dumbly at Frank.

"'Bout halfway to nowhere in particular," chuckled Boone. "Feelin' any better?"

"Yeah . . . Except for the pounding in my head—"

"Do you think you kin walk on your own now?" asked Frank. "The trail's much flatter here."

"I . . . I . . . I'll try."

The soldiers shouldered their weapons and trudged along downriver until the skies opened up again. The wind roared, and the rain fell in sheets until the men could no longer see or keep their footing. Finally, Colonel Kane bellowed, "Okay, men! Fall out! Make camp!"

Bucky and the other hunters swarmed onto a wide bench to the left of the trail and immediately began hacking boughs from the nearest hemlocks with their hatchets and knives. Jimmy watched in a stupor while his friends wove the boughs together into the rainproof roof of a lean-to. The lumberjacks made similar shelters out of windfalls and dead logs. In less than an hour the whole company was billeted in an impromptu village. Plenty of dead pine branches stayed dry beneath the forest canopy, and the soldiers used this wood to build roaring fires beside their huts.

Bucky, Boone, Frank, and Jimmy huddled together inside their shelter. Although wrapped in Bucky's wool blanket, Jimmy's teeth chattered so violently Boone said, "You make more noise than a chilled beaver. Why don't you slide closer to the fire?"

"Yeah, you'll warm your bones in no time," assured Frank.

After Jimmy did what he was told, Bucky slid beside him and whispered, "I got real mad at you last night when you flew off the handle an' got drunk like you did. I think you done a bad thing."

"Oh?"

"An' now that you're feelin' better . . . I wanted to talk to you 'bout your mother."

Jimmy swallowed hard and fidgeted with the blanket. "What about her?" he bleated.

"Don't you think it's time to patch things up with her some? Write her a letter at least?"

"Why? So she can say I'm still her mama's boy?"

"Jimmy, she jess loves you so much . . . she kinda goes too far in showin' it. Can't you at least write a note tellin' her you're all right?"

"I . . . I . . . I could do that."

"I'll bet the colonel has some paper you could use—"

"Okay! Okay! I'll go see him as soon as I'm warm enough."

"Tell your mother . . . I said 'hello.' "

"Hey, what are you two whisperin' about?" joshed Boone from the back of the lean-to. "Plannin' to desert?"

"Nothin' like that," said Bucky. "We're jess wishin'—for a nice hot meal."

"Hey, can't have everything," chuckled Frank. "At least we're out of the rain."

"And now that we are," said Bucky, "I think I better tend to my Kentuck rifle."

"Yeah, me too," agreed Boone.

"Don't want my gun rustin' up, neither," added Frank.

The three soldiers disassembled their rifles and dug pieces of cloth from their hunting bags. While unfouling their barrels of caked black powder and rainwater, they boasted and laughed and tried to top each other's hunting stories.

"We all know how Boone, here, earned his name," joshed Frank, after spinning an exaggerated tale. "I always wondered how you got yours, Bucky."

"Pa named me for his blood brother who saved his life. Then I killed a bear that was after him."

"No, really," laughed Boone. "You can tell us."

"I jess did."

"Well, you musta been mighty strong to have strangled that bear, 'cause you couldn'ta been more than a babe when you done it," howled Boone.

"I never said I strangled it. I shot it chargin'. It weren't more than a step away from Pa at the time."

"An' I thought Boone told some whoppers," needled Frank.

Jimmy felt forgotten as the others joked and oiled their weapons. Finally, he crawled to his feet and said, "Excuse me a minute, fellas. I . . . I . . . I gotta go see the colonel."

"Goin' to turn in your drum?" snickered Boone. "Shucks! I thought you was finally havin' some fun."

Jimmy replied with a barrage of off-color slang he had learned from the lumberjacks and then ducked out of the lean-to. The rain had slackened to a drizzle, and he made his way across the encampment to the colonel's tent, where a lantern flickered. There was a guard posted at the tent entrance, and Jimmy said to him, "If Colonel Kane isn't busy, may I have a word—"

"Come in, Jewett," boomed Kane's voice through the canvas wall.

Startled, Jimmy entered the colonel's quarters to find the officer wiping his saber and pistol with oily rags. Jimmy saluted shyly and then said, "Excuse me, sir, but I was wondering if you might have some paper and a pen. I want to write to . . . to my mother."

"Certainly, son. I encourage all my soldiers to keep in touch with their loved ones. A man's family is more important than anything else in the world. Later this evening I plan to write to my own dear wife. You're welcome to remain here where it's dry and compose your letter. Here, sit over by the lantern so you can see."

"Thank you, sir."

Colonel Kane dug some paper, a quill pen, and a bottle of ink out of his saddle bags and handed them to Jimmy. The boy squatted on a stump in the corner of the tent to scrawl in a shaky hand:

Dear Mother,

　　I'm camping out in the woods near Driftwood. It rained all day. We just built a lean-to to sleep in tonight. We have been marching a long time. It was hard at first, but my legs don't hurt so much now. I made some new friends and had some real adventures. Bucky says hi. He wanted me to write so you know we're both ok.

　　　　　　　　　　　　Jimmy

Jimmy waved the letter until the ink was dry and folded it. After he scrawled the address on the back of the paper, the colonel said, "I'll be glad to seal your letter for you and mail it when we reach Driftwood. If any of the other men wish to write, tell them to come see me."

"Thank you, sir. I know that my mother will be grateful. I'll tell my friends about your offer."

Chapter Fifteen

A Driftwood Welcome

It was the twenty-fourth of April when Colonel Kane led his company of McKean County riflemen to the rafting place on the Sinnemahoning known as Driftwood. The valley had gradually widened all morning, and in the distance the men had seen a long sloping hogback that cut the horizon at a twenty-degree angle. This was the landmark they had been watching for. Where this ridge dropped to meet the valley floor marked the point the Bennett Branch dumped into the Sinnemahoning, making the river deep enough for travel other than by canoe. The Bucktails fired their guns into the air and whooped for joy when they saw that their long march was about to end.

Bucky and Jimmy chattered excitedly when they marched down a steep slope into the grand, booming village of Driftwood. Never before had either of them seen seventy-two buildings in one location. Besides the usual homes, there were four hotels, two churches, three schools, a general store, an opera house, a theater, and several taverns. A Mr. Cochran owned everything in sight, and his surname was prominent on many of the signs.

There was also a brand-new railroad station in Driftwood. Colonel Kane's eyes lit up when he saw it. He was about to comment on its magnificence to Captain Blanchard when he noticed that there were no train tracks laid down in front of it.

"It looks like we'll have to build rafts, after all," the colonel muttered to the captain.

"I figured as much," groaned Blanchard.

Colonel Kane had no sooner paraded his troops into the center of town when he climbed up on the balcony of the most prestigious hotel to address the citizens of Driftwood. "Ladies and gentlemen," he began, "these valiant men of the newly formed Bucktail Regiment have trekked over fifty miles of treacherous wilderness to be with you today. Without a railroad to transport them to war, they are now forced to build rafts to carry them downriver. Rafts require lumber. Lumber costs money. All these men have are their rifles and the clothes on their backs. I beseech you in the name of the precious Union that they go off to defend, to help them in their need. Officers will be passing their hats among you. Please donate any money you can spare for the cause of freedom. Step up! Be the first to contribute! Please! Help send these brave men to defend Pennsylvania against the Rebel menace!"

Colonel Kane's speech ended in an explosion of cheers and gunfire. Captain Blanchard, Lieutenant Ward, and Lieutenant Rice immediately began passing their hats. They worked their way through the frenzied crowd. They sought contributions in the hotel bars where they knew the drunks would be most generous of all. Within twenty minutes the officers returned to their colonel with their hats overflowing with silver pieces and pocket change.

Colonel Kane held up the hatsful of money, and the citizens roared and applauded themselves. The colonel bellowed a hearty "thank you" on behalf of the regiment and said to the officers, "Your help is appreciated, gentlemen. Captain, march the men to the outskirts of town to bivouac. Keep them busy. We don't want them slipping off to the taverns. I'll go now to see about purchasing timber. Lieutenants, follow me."

Blanchard saluted and returned to the town square to roughly order the men back into their ranks. "Gol-dang officers. I need a little nip after all that hikin'," mumbled Sergeant Curtis under his breath.

"Sergeant!" barked Blanchard. "Quit your bellyaching! Get your men in line! Hurry up!"

Colonel Kane, meanwhile, trailed by the two lieutenants, strode up the street to the office of Mr. Cochran's lumber company. Inside, they set their three hatsful of change on the counter as a large clerk with little squinty eyes rose from behind a desk. The man wore a handlebar mustache and a derby hat, and his smile broadened with greed when he asked, "What can I do for you fine gentlemen?"

"We need enough timber to build four good-sized rafts," said the colonel evenly.

"Timber we got," replied the clerk. "If you're willin' to cut it. It's growing over yonder on Thunder Mountain. I'll just count up your money an' send a company fella with you. He'll show you how much and where to cut."

"And I'll have one of my officers help you count," barked the colonel. "What is the exact price per board foot?"

"Well, that often varies with the season and demand," answered the clerk. "Don't you gentlemen worry none. Being you're army an' all, I'll make sure you get a special rate."

"My men are the best marksmen in these parts," reminded Kane with a meaningful glare. "I'd remember that while you're doing your ciphering."

"Mr. Cochran owns everything here in Driftwood. I would keep that in mind if I were you, sir. We also got axes and crosscut saws your soldiers can use. That costs extra."

Colonel Kane returned fuming to camp with his two lieutenants and a half-drunk agent from Cochran's office. The agent had a patch over one eye and walked with a severe limp. His good eye had a shifty look that made the colonel uneasy.

Colonel Kane assembled the men and divided them into two groups. The lumbermen of his company would harvest the timber, while the hunters would trim it and skid it to the river's edge. The soldiers were sluggish from their long morning hike, and many were angry about being denied liberty. It took a lot of cursing from Captain Blanchard and his lieutenants to get the men moving up Thunder Mountain.

Despite their initial grumbles, the lumbermen went to work with a vengeance once the agent issued them double-edged axes and two-man crosscut saws from a company shed. With familiar tools in their hands, they were a force to be dealt with, and the burly men were whistling tavern songs in no time while they hacked and sawed tirelessly at hemlock trunks. They actually seemed disappointed when the agent signaled for them to stop. It didn't seem possible that all the coins in those three hats had purchased such a small section of timber.

All limbs had to be pruned from the logs before they could be moved down to the river. Bucky, Jimmy, Boone, and Frank were with Lieutenant Ward's party assigned to this job. Jimmy had never used an ax of any kind, and he was wringing with sweat after a few minutes' labor. His arms were so rubbery it affected his aim. Twice he almost cut off his foot. With another errant ax stroke, he barely missed Boone's hand. Finally, Bucky said, "Hey, Jimmy, why don't you put down the ax and haul away the branches we cut off."

"Yeah," wheezed Boone, "if I'm gonna get wounded, I'd rather Johnny Reb done it. Not somebody from my own company."

"Okay," panted Jimmy, leaning on his ax. "Just give me a minute to catch my breath. I don't know how much longer I could hold on to this handle, anyway. My blisters got blisters."

"Hey, Jewett! Get back to work!" barked Lieutenant Ward. "We have a lot more trees to trim before dark. I don't care if you're the drummer boy, or not. Everyone has to pull his weight in my outfit."

And pull their weight they did until it was too dark to see what they were chopping or hauling. Not even Brewer or Sergeant Curtis tried sneaking away for a drink when the company was finally ordered to return to camp. The officers were watching too closely for any of the soldiers to stray. The lieutenants acted like shepherds on a stormy night and dogged their men through the lamplit streets.

While Bucky, Boone, and Jimmy stumbled half asleep past one of the hotels, a burly bartender called to Jimmy through the swinging doors of the barroom, "Hey, sonny," he chirped. "Come on in, an' have a drink on the house. It'll make a man of you—"

"No thank you," Jimmy replied with a queasy grin. "I already became a man back in Emporium."

Chapter Sixteen

BRAWLING WITH DOWNHOMERS

The next morning it was still only half-light when the officers began rooting the men out of their blankets. After a breakfast of diluted coffee, the company was herded down to the river bank to begin work on four rafts. The sleepy soldiers filled the dawn with oaths while they wrestled with the heavy logs and their heavier eyelids.

Raft building was a familiar occupation to the lumbermen of the company, and they barked orders to the hunters until they became familiar with the process. The hunters soon learned that the larger rafts were constructed in three sections. Each of these sections was twenty logs wide, with longer logs used for the middle portion.

Bucky and Boone tied the logs of one of the end sections together with rope bought at Mr. Cochran's general store. Frank and Jimmy attached braces with wooden pegs to the top and bottom of both ends. Jimmy was about as good with a hammer as he had been with an ax the night before. After he had dropped more pegs than he'd pounded into place, Curtis howled, "You gotta be the gol-dang clumsiest soldier in this here Union army!"

"S-S-Sorry, Sergeant. I'm not doing it on purpose. I'm just as anxious to get these rafts done as you are."

"I doubt that, sonny boy," growled Curtis.

While Bucky and the others helped line up the three sections and began tying them together with more rope,

Jimmy asked, "Wouldn't it have been easier to build one big raft rather than fiddle around with these three pieces?"

"What we's trying to do, sonny boy," said Curtis, "is to build a flexible transport that will bend with the rapids. Anything more solid would bust apart goin' over the first waterfall we come to."

"Jewett!" snapped Brewer. "Why don't you quit runnin' your mouth and get back here and help me build the outhouse for our raft. After that, we gotta make a steerin' oar for each end."

While the Bucktails hustled to finish the first of their transports, across the Sinnemahoning they spotted a column of men moving toward them. "It's the boys from Elk County!" shouted Colonel Kane, as the faint strains of "Yankee Doodle" wafted upriver. "They've come from Bennett's Valley. They're right on time!"

The company marched smartly up the opposite bank and across the Driftwood bridge. When they stood at attention before the colonel, Sergeant Curtis stopped work on one of the rudder oars long enough to spit into the river and chortle, "Hey, look at the little fellas they got playing them drums and fifes."

"Why, they's even scrawnier than Jewett," scoffed Brewer.

"What'd they do? Go an' enlist a bunch of gol-dang choir boys? Not one of 'em can be over eleven."

"Half of them with rifles ain't any older."

"Look at the baby face on that one."

"Does he call that a beard?" howled Curtis. "I seed more hair on a porcupine."

"Why didn't they stay home with mama?"

"Hell, mama's probably ashamed of them puny fellas!"

"Them Elk County babes will be down with the colic before we even get started for Lock Haven."

Again Curtis spit into the river as the new troops rushed to the log pile to begin work on a second raft. It took a multitude of their men to move one log, and the sergeant laughed and cursed at their lack of strength. It was soon evident that the Elk County recruits weren't lumbermen, so Curtis was ordered to direct them. Even then, their raft was so ineptly constructed that the McKean County Company had to redo their work.

By midday Captain Blanchard's men were irritable as bears waking from hibernation. Not only were they worn out from their heavy labor, but they also hadn't eaten a decent meal in two days. They cursed and snarled at the Elk County troops until Colonel Kane decided it was time to relieve the growing tension. "Culp, Crossmire, Crandall!" barked the colonel. "Take some hunters downriver and see if you can shoot us some fresh meat."

"Yes, sir," echoed Bucky and his friends.

"You boys from Bennett Valley look like fishermen," continued Kane. "Why don't you go upriver and snag us some trout?"

"You bet, sir."

"Sergeant Curtis. You're doing a fine job on these rafts. You and your McKean workmen can fall out and get some rest."

"Thank you, sir!"

An hour later, the hunters returned with a huge elk and two fat deer. Roaring fires were started, and each of the animals was cooked whole on a spit. The fishermen contributed several baskets of brookies to the feast, and two hundred men gorged on game until the twinkle returned to their half-starved eyes.

While Sergeant Curtis gnawed contentedly on a haunch of venison, he said to the Elk County boys at his fire, "You fellas gotta be the weakest woodsmen I ever seed. You handle logs like a bunch of gol-dang dancing girls. Ain't you downhomers ever built nothin' before?"

"Maybe we ain't big lumber butchers like you," replied a scrawny soldier from Bennett's Valley, "but we can whip our weight in wildcats."

"Well, I reckon if you fight like you build rafts, old Johnny Reb ain't got much to worry about."

"Maybe you'd like to find out fer yourself, McKean man!"

The soldier tossed aside a half-eaten hunk of venison loin and leaped at Curtis with a snarl. The sergeant swatted away his attacker like a mosquito, only to be beset by five other Elk County men. When Brewer saw his friend go down in a pile of thrashing limbs, he leaped up and began kicking the exposed ribs of the top assailant. This brought more downhomers into the fray, followed by Curtis' lumberjack buddies. Pretty soon, the whole camp was in an uproar as the fracas spread from fire to fire. There were plenty of busted lips and black eyes before the officers regained order with the flats of their swords. Curtis and two Bennett's Valley men still did not stop punching each other until Colonel Kane fired a warning shot from his pistol.

"If you boys fight the Rebs with the same vigor you fight each other, we'll win the war in a month!" bellowed the colonel, with his beard bristling like an angry Scotch terrier. "Who is responsible for this brawl? Speak up! Otherwise, all of you will be marching double time around this camp with knapsacks full of rocks on your backs!"

Colonel Kane paused for a moment to survey the ranks. When no one volunteered to explain the scuffle, he whirled around to confront the usual instigator. "So, *Corporal* Curtis," Kane barked with a menacing glare, "you'd rather let the whole company suffer than fess up. Dinner is over. We still have a few hours of daylight left. Let's get cracking on those rafts!"

Curtis muttered something under his breath about downhomers and then vented his rage razing the bark from logs for the colonel's personal transport. This raft would be smaller than the others and would have a corral built on it for Old Glencoe. Curtis figured that if he took special care in its construction, that Colonel Kane would promote him back to sergeant. The only problem was, Curtis and his workmen ran out of lumber after only one of the two sections of the raft was complete.

"Hey, boys," winked Corporal Curtis, "didn't you remember seeing an extra pile of timber at the foot of Thunder Mountain when we came through there last night? It seems a shame that all them good logs are just layin' there rottin' away."

"Yeah, they would just about finish up the colonel's raft," chuckled Brewer, "if'n there was just somebody to fetch 'em down here."

"What'll you say we go and borrow a few of them logs," suggested the corporal. "Hell, nobody'll ever miss 'em. I'll bet the colonel hisself would give us orders to do jess that if he was here."

"We ain't stealin' no timber," grunted one of the men Curtis had thumped in the dinner brawl. "You got us in enough trouble already."

"What do you mean you won't go!" thundered the corporal.

"Us Elk men ain't thieves," added another soldier. "If you McKean boys wanna rob Mr. Cochran, you can go without us."

Curtis growled threateningly and immediately led his squad back to Thunder Mountain. Just as the corporal had remembered, there were twenty-odd piles of logs strewn about, ripe for the taking. With a trained eye, the McKean lumberjacks chose only the best timber. They lifted a few trees from each pile and made no unnecessary noise to avoid detection.

Curtis and his lumberjack cronies had no sooner skidded the logs back to the river and had begun to assemble them than the limping agent from Mr. Cochran's office showed up at Colonel Kane's tent and sought an audience. Moments later, Kane came storming down to the riverbank with

Cochran's man in tow. His eyes glowed like fanned coals when he barked, "Corporal Curtis!"

"Yes, Colonel?"

"Captain Blanchard told me awhile ago that you didn't have enough timber to finish my raft."

"Well, sir, awhile ago we didn't."

"Then where did *this* lumber come from?"

"U-U-Um, me and my men . . . just happened across it—"

"On Mister Cochran's land," finished the agent.

"What do you mean?" asked Curtis.

"I mean you stole it!"

"Stole it, my foot!" howled the corporal, hopping mad. "Beg your pardon, Colonel, but he's the only crook around here. I've bought ten times the timber for the money you gave him yesterday."

"Well, *Private* Curtis, all I know is that you took those logs from posted land. Until I get this worked out with Mr. Cochran, you'll have to stop building my raft."

Colonel Kane turned and followed the agent through the streets of Driftwood to a sprawling wooden mansion adorned with a pillared porch. On the porch sat a slight man in a gray sack coat and plaid trousers. He wore a black silk cravat and was sipping on a glass of imported Scotch whiskey. He motioned for the colonel to take a seat in an exquisitely carved rocking chair and offered him a drink.

"No, thank you," replied Kane, emphasizing the words with a curt nod. "Are you Mr. Cochran?"

"Yes, Colonel, and we have a little matter to discuss concerning some stolen timber."

"I apologize, sir, for the overzealous nature of my men. The culprit responsible has been punished, as your agent can testify."

"That's fine and dandy," replied Cochran, "but it don't pay for the lumber. You either have your men return it to me or pay for it with cash money."

"But we have no more money," said Kane. "Where is your patriotic spirit, sir?"

"You have a fine, spirited horse, Colonel. Maybe if you would leave him here, I would overlook the theft of a little lumber."

"No! I would never part with Old Glencoe."

"Then I must insist on the money."

"I already told you. I have none. Although I can't pay you now, what I can promise you is some very lucrative future business. Once the railroad connects Driftwood with the village I built to the north, there will be plenty of opportunity for men like us to trade commodities that will mutually benefit our two towns."

"What if you go off and get yourself killed? Then, how much trading are you going to do?"

"Here is my pocket watch, Mr. Cochran. It's over a hundred years old and a Kane family heirloom. It's yours if I don't come back to claim it after the war."

"I think you just got yourself the timber you needed," said Cochran with a slippery smile.

"Even if I did pay ten times more than it's worth," replied the colonel.

Chapter Seventeen

The Wild Raft Ride

Construction continued on Colonel Kane's fleet of transports at first light. Although the officers really pushed the men, it wasn't until midday that the four rafts were ready to embark. The Sinnemahoning was a twisting rattlesnake of a river, full of frothing rapids, dangerous drop-offs, and boulder fangs. This necessitated that the little flotilla travel single file after pushing off from the bank to the martial strains of fife and drum and the halloing of the Driftwood citizenry. These were the same townsfolk who the day before had cautioned the colonel against sending scouts ahead. "Too dangerous!" the local loggers had hissed. "Too many mountain lions downriver!"

Colonel Kane's raft led the way down the treacherous Sinnemahoning. Constructed of two sections, it was the smallest of the four transports. It was also the most well-built, with a railing surrounding its sides and a corral for Old Glencoe taking up a good portion of its deck. A green hickory pole, graced with a bucktail and the Stars and Stripes, served as a flagstaff. The crew of the raft was made up of fifteen of the strongest men in the regiment. They stood watchfully at the railings with long poles ready to fend off jagged rocks that protruded from the stream bed. Piloting the rear steering oar was Smith Guthrie, who made gigantic Brewer look like a runt.

Each of the other rafts carried a hundred men. Made in three sections, they bent with each dip in the river. The Cameron County company, having arrived earlier that morning, manned the second transport. They were fresh from their homes and the most knowledgeable of river rafting. If Colonel Kane's vessel floundered, the Cameron men would be the best suited to come to its aid.

The McKean County soldiers steered the third craft, while the Elk County transport brought up the rear. For the men of Elk and McKean white water rafting was an unwanted adventure, and they howled and cursed as the rapids buffeted them with frothing fists of spray. Most of them huddled white-faced away from the sides of their bucking rafts and accepted pole duty only when physically threatened by their officers.

Private Curtis was at the helm of raft three, and he spit into the river each time he narrowly missed a foaming boulder. He was too busy steering to jeer at Bucky and Jimmy, who quaked with fear at his feet. Even powerful Brewer looked rattled as he struggled to maintain his balance and push them from danger with his pole. "What you staring at?" he snarled at Jimmy after a particularly close call.

After the fleet plunged through a long shoot of rapids, it bobbed along a deep pool that allowed the men to catch their breath and take in the wild scenery of the Sinnemahoning Valley. Deer grazed everywhere along the banks, and water snakes of great length swam past them without fear. Above them the sky was filled with circling buzzards that made Bucky cringe superstitiously.

As the rafts drifted lazily through the calm pool, Bucky heard a faint roar from downriver. "What's that?" he wondered aloud, straining to listen.

"What's what?" asked Jimmy with a sick smile.

"That noise!"

When they floated around the next bend, Bucky could see mist rising from the river ahead. Near the tail of the pool, they were again gripped by a powerful current that sped them along to likely doom. Bucky watched several soldiers in the lead raft scramble to force Old Glencoe down on his knees. "Hold on!" Bucky shouted when he saw Curtis brace himself and grip the rudder oar with both hands.

One by one the rafts were airborne over an eight-foot waterfall that silenced even the most vulgar-tongued men of the regiment. Many crossed themselves, while others prayed in midair for their deliverance. Bucky watched the first two transports splash down and disappear in a wall of white water. It wasn't until he was flying over the falls that he saw Colonel Kane's raft emerge from the spray.

Bucky's raft hit the river below with such force that he was thrown headlong into a squirming pile of men. The transport buckled violently, but somehow the ropes held the three sections together. A numbing wave of icy water crashed down on them as they plunged out of control. Finally, Curtis righted himself and gripped the rudder with a power only terror can produce. Bucky dared not look up until the water receded and he felt the raft straighten in the current.

Bucky rose half-drowned from a writhing mass of men to find Jimmy lying unconscious on the deck beside him. Jimmy had a nasty bruise on his forehead, and his breathing was short and erratic. Bucky rolled his friend onto his belly and clapped him on the back until he choked and spluttered.

"W-W-What happened?" asked Jimmy, when he finally sat up and shook his head.

"We made it," grinned Bucky as he patted his friend reassuringly on the shoulder. "That's all you need to know."

Colonel Kane motioned the other rafts to shore after he saw that each had survived its plunge over the waterfall. The fleet was secured with mooring ropes, and bonfires were built to dry out the soggy, frightened men. It was now late afternoon, and Colonel Kane said to his captains, "We might as well camp here for the night. There's no use taking further risks with soldiers too shaken to think straight. Have the boys tighten the raft ropes and gather firewood. That should take their minds off our misadventure."

"Yes, sir."

The fires leaped merrily in the growing gloom until curses and insults echoed from the relaxing soldiers. "Boy, what a ride that was," Frank Crandall moaned, while nursing a bruised shoulder.

"I thought it was great!" crowed Boone. "When we shot over that waterfall, it was like breakin' a headstrong horse. I don't know if Old Glencoe liked it much, though. I heard he was pretty hard to control once they splashed back into the river."

"If you was havin' so much fun," wondered Private Curtis, "why did you have your eyes closed so much?"

"I heard him squealing like a gal who seed her first rattlesnake," scoffed Brewer. "What a joke!"

"Hey, big man. You looked pretty green around the gills, too," reminded Frank.

"Yeah, that was because all you sissy boys made me sick."

"Bucky? W-W-What did you think of our trip?" asked Jimmy after Curtis and Brewer moved on to another fire to insult the Elk County troops.

"I ain't afraid to admit it. I was scared to death. Let's just go to sleep an' get a fresh start tomorrow."

The night was a restless one for Bucky. The shrieks of a panther exploded from his dreams, and twice he woke with a start when something skulked through the shadowy brush. He was about to have a look around until he saw how peacefully Jimmy snored beside him. Still, as a precaution, Bucky piled a few more logs on the fire. Feeling anxious, he reloaded his rifle with a fresh charge of powder and replaced the percussion cap. He had seen first-hand what wolves can do to a man. He didn't want to find out the hard way about mountain lions.

At daybreak, the Bucktails were again assembled on their rafts. When they were about to cast off, Bucky caught sight of the very panther that had troubled his dreams. The big cat slunk through the brush toward the river, and Bucky eased his rifle to his shoulder. The beast was nine feet long and as black as the night it haunted. Its fierce eyes glowed with menace. It had come for its usual morning drink and wasn't happy with the human interlopers who stood between it and the water.

Brewer was still ashore untying the mooring rope when he noticed the beast snarling at him from the beech. "Here, kitty, kitty," he mocked, while the panther edged still closer. "Just 'cause I got a bucktail in my hat don't mean you—"

Before Brewer could finish his quip, the giant cat leaped on him and planted its claws in the middle of his chest. Brewer let out a surprised yelp and toppled over backward with the panther biting and slashing for his jugular. Only Bucky's snap shot saved his life. Brewer rolled gasping from the dying animal and clutched his throat in a vulnerable way.

"Nice shot!" applauded Captain Blanchard, slapping Bucky on the shoulder. "Drilled that critter right through the head! How did you do that without aiming?"

"Just lucky, I guess, Captain."

Brewer gave the dead panther a kick and finished untying the mooring rope.

"Hey, you owe him one," Curtis shouted as his friend jumped back onto the raft.

"I don't owe that stinkin' Injun nothin'," grunted Brewer. "I didn't ask him to help me. Why, I'da killed that panther with my bare hands if he hadn't interfered."

"Yeah, right. You're such a tough man," scoffed Jimmy until Brewer silenced him with a withering glare.

"Come on, let's shove off," said Brewer as he swaggered to the far side of the raft. "We got a river to fight today."

Even Curtis just shook his head when the tangle-bearded giant wouldn't acknowledge that Bucky had saved his life.

While his pole men pushed and grunted, he worked the rudder until the raft moved straight down the main current and into another chute of rock-strewn rapids.

Bucky had just finished reloading his rifle when he noticed Brewer glaring at him from the edge of the raft. "What's wrong with you?" he finally asked the giant out of exasperation. "What did I ever do to make you hate me so much?"

Brewer slammed his pole down on the deck and charged Bucky before the boy could react. The man growled, leaped on his enemy, and rolled with him back and forth across the pitching raft. The combatants had their hands locked around each other's windpipes. In their struggle they smashed into Curtis, knocking the rudder oar from its housing. Immediately, the raft went out of control and was sucked by the swift current into an island of jagged rock. The transport splintered on impact, hurling its passengers into the icy water.

Brewer and Bucky were still choking each other when the collision tumbled them into the river. They hit with a heavy splash that sucked their breath away. The giant surfaced sputtering, but did not allow Bucky to come up for air. He continued to hold the boy's head under the water until Bucky's vision was clouded with darkness. In panic-fueled rage, Bucky lashed out with his legs, pummeling Brewer in the solar plexus. The giant gasped and loosened his grip, allowing Bucky to break free and gulp in some oxygen. Before Brewer could relocate his enemy, the current swept him into the island rocks where it smashed him like a rag doll. He threw up his arms in shocked surprise and then sank into the icy depths.

Bucky floated along, letting the current drag him from danger. He kicked his legs to stay afloat and paddled a little with his frozen hands. He was too numb to think of anything but his own survival.

The Cameron County men anchored as soon as they saw the third transport break into pieces. When Bucky drew even with their raft, a burly lumberjack held out his pole, and the half-drowned boy desperately latched on to it. He was hauled up on the deck and found himself sprawled next to Jimmy. His friend had been pulled out of the river just moments before.

Bucky lay hugging the deck with his eyes closed. His neck was covered with giant welts and blood leaked from a deep gash on his cheek. His blue lips shivered uncontrollably until two soldiers took turns rubbing Bucky's limbs and then wrapped him in a wool blanket. Why, Brewer? Why? the boy kept thinking while the soldiers worked on him. Why couldn't you jess once have accepted the help . . . of an Indian?

Bucky continued to shiver. Finally, his blurry vision focused on the Kentucky rifle Jimmy cradled in his arms. "T-T-That's Pa's gun," stammered Bucky through chattering teeth. "You saved it. H-H-How can I ever thank you?"

"Thank the Lord," said Jimmy. "He's the One Who saved our lives. The rifle slid right into my lap when I went over the side. I couldn't let it get lost once I saw it was yours."

Before Bucky could reply, one of the Cameron County men shouted, "Look, the last raft can't make it around the wreck! They're stuck!"

Chapter Eighteen

Mangled, Mashed, and Mutilated

The midsection of the splintered raft lodged itself sideways between two rocks in the main channel of the Sinnemahoning. The Elk County transport whipped down the current and smashed head-on into the wreckage. Several soldiers, including the helmsman, were sent sprawling to the deck. No matter how hard the pole men pushed, they could not dislodge the obstacle from the channel.

"What are we gonna do, Captain Winslow?" shrieked a pale lieutenant above the roar of the river.

"Why don't we send a couple of men with hatchets onto the wreck?" suggested a stocky sergeant. "Me an' Deke'll go. Won't take much to hack apart the ropes that's holdin' her together."

"Too dangerous!" barked Winslow. "If it broke up all at once, you boys would get swept under them logs and drowned."

"If only we had a keg of black powder," shouted the lieutenant, "we could blow her out of the way!"

"Well, we don't! All we can do is steer into that eddy over yonder!" yelled the captain.

"What good'll that do, sir? The water ain't deep enough for us to get through."

"Then we'll just have to take our raft apart, move her below the wreck, an' put her back together."

The pole men grunted, pushed, and swore until they dislodged the Elk County transport from where it was trapped against the smashed McKean craft. They shoved their raft sideways through the raging current until it ran aground in the shallows several feet from shore. Then the whole company leaped into the icy water and wrestled with their lightened vessel until it rested against the bank.

As the Elk soldiers worked feverishly to disassemble their raft, the Cameron crew moored their transport behind Colonel Kane's. Soon bonfires were roaring all along the shore, and the half-frozen McKean men huddled close to the flames. Jimmy, Bucky, Boone, and Frank shivered near one fire, rubbing their limbs and stripping off their drenched shirts. "I . . . I . . . I d-don't know about you b-b-boys," said Frank through chattering teeth, "b-b-but I . . . I . . . I h-h-hope we s-s-stay here the r-r-rest of the d-d-day."

"It should take the Elk boys some time to untie all them logs," said Boone. "They's gonna have to dry out, too."

"Hey, at least we d-d-didn't l-l-lose our r-r-rifles," stuttered Frank.

"Or our l-l-l-lives," reminded Jimmy.

"Now all we gotta do is figure out how our company's gonna fit on the other three rafts," said Boone. "I sure don't wanna get stranded in this valley!"

Bucky and his friends continued to warm themselves when a whoop went up from the river. A squad of Cameron County men squinted and pointed to the rapids and leaped onto their raft to fetch some long poles. Soon they were sprinting off downstream like hounds on a fresh coon scent. Several times they stopped to jab into the current before rushing off again down the riverbank.

After several minutes another yell reverberated through camp. Bucky heard Jimmy gasp and turned to see the Cameron squad trudging from the brush lugging Brewer's corpse. The big logger's skull was split like a melon. His face was smashed to jam, and one of his eyes was poked out. His stained teeth were exposed in a hideous grin. One arm dangled broken at the elbow. One foot was twisted almost off. He was mangled, mashed, and mutilated by a force even more ferocious than his own anger.

"We saw him bobbin' in the river!" exclaimed one of the Cameron men when Colonel Kane and the McKean Company gathered to examine the body.

"How could that be?" asked Bucky. "I . . . I . . . I saw him sink like a stone after he . . . fell off our raft . . . an' smashed against some rocks."

"Musta been hung up on a snag upriver an' then busted loose," puffed another Cameron soldier. "He's a heavy un, he is."

"I still can't figure out how you McKean men wrecked," said Colonel Kane. "Can any of you explain it to me?"

Bucky stared at his feet, and his friends squirmed uncomfortably next to him. Finally, Lieutenant Ward said, "Me and Captain Blanchard were sittin' near the front of the raft, sir, when it suddenly went out of control. All we know is that there was some kind of ruckus going on near the helmsman, Private Curtis."

"Curtis, what exactly did happen?" asked Colonel Kane.

Curtis stared glumly at Brewer's broken body. He swallowed hard and then muttered, "We hit a rock, an' Brewer lost his footin', sir. He landed on top of Culp. When they tried to untangle theirselves, they knocked loose the rudder oar."

"So, it was an accident?"

"Yes, sir!"

"How about you, Private Culp? Do you have anything to add?"

"No, Colonel."

"Anybody else?"

"We're jess thankful we only lost one man," said Boone.

"Amen!" enthused Jimmy.

"Well, it's time we give Private Brewer here a proper burial," replied Colonel Kane. "And let's get it done now before the big cats come out. We don't have any shovels, but sharp sticks should dig up this soil."

The Cameron squad helped Bucky, Curtis, and the others gouge a shallow grave in the black woods dirt. The McKean men forgot all about being cold once they began digging like gophers. When the hole was three feet deep, they wrapped the dead giant in a blanket and lowered him into the earth. Then Colonel Kane returned from his tent and respectfully removed his hat. The assembly followed suit as the colonel offered these words, "Men, we've lost Private Thaddeus Brewer, the first Bucktail to fall in our great cause. I know he was a man of strong feelings, one of which was hate, but we must not dwell there. We must remember that Private Brewer was a willing soldier who believed, as we do, in preserving the Union. May God rest his soul."

When Kane had finished, Jimmy asked, "Sir, can I say a few words from the Bible? I know it real good because my father's a preacher."

"Son, I can think of nothing better."

"Lord," Jimmy began. "Brewer was tough, and he was mean to Bucky and me. But we hold no grudge. We're sorry for the way things turned out. Please, God, take the soul of this man into Your house of many mansions. As it says, Lord, in Ecclesiastes, 'All go unto one place; all are of the dust and all turn to dust again.' Amen."

"Amen," murmured the Bucktails. Several soldiers pointed their rifles into the air and fired a salute to their drowned comrade. Some crossed themselves. All kept their heads bowed until the shots echoed away into the distance.

While the rest of the company filed back to camp, Bucky, Curtis, Frank, and Boone filled in the grave and covered it with stones to keep it safe from animals. Jimmy, meanwhile, fashioned a simple cross from two pieces of log that had washed ashore from the splintered raft.

"Why didn't you tell the colonel about Brewer and me fightin'?" asked Bucky as he helped Curtis roll a rock on top of the grave.

"Brewer was stubborn and meanspirited," grunted Curtis, "but he was my friend. Ain't no use stirrin' up trouble for somebody who's gone."

"I pray that we can . . . stop feuding now," said Jimmy with a hopeful smile.

"Well," replied Curtis evenly, "at least I can thank you fellas for helping me lay my friend to rest."

That night was an uneasy one for the whole company. It turned unseasonably cold, and a few snowflakes tumbled from the pitch-black skies. Most of the men were too chilled to sleep. They sat murmuring around their fires discussing the funeral and the accident that could have killed them all. Some wondered at the terrible power of the river. More than a few prayed for a safe passage to Harrisburg.

Every time Bucky closed his eyes, he saw the battered face of the tangle-bearded giant. That and the snarl of a prowling panther made him so edgy that Frank finally said, "If you're still thinkin' about Brewer, you gotta stop. He got what was comin' to him."

"That's right," added Boone. "It was either him or you. It was mighty scary seein' him all busted up like that, but you can bet he ain't the only corpse we're gonna run across before we gets home again."

As soon as it was light enough to see, Colonel Kane ordered every available man to work on the Elk County craft. Although just a private, Curtis was put in charge, and he soon had crews organized to drag the logs downriver and reassemble them.

After the three sections of the raft were tied back together, the colonel said, "Men, I want you to board your usual transports. Half of the McKean Company can ride with me. The other half will be divided between the Cameron and Elk vessels. Let's go!"

Bucky and his friends squirmed onto the Cameron raft. There were so many soldiers crowded onto the deck that the pole men hardly had room to step when they pushed off from shore. The teeming raft sat so low the men were doused with spray at the slightest dip in the river. Soaked and shivering, they soon ignored their grumbling stomachs that hadn't been fed in two days.

The transports bucked through one set of rapids after another. The ropes strained and the logs creaked at each new challenge. Twice, the front section of the Cameron craft bent so severely that Bucky was sure it would snap off. He wondered if the horrific pitching came close to what Brewer must have experienced in his ride to hell.

After Kane's little fleet lurched over a three-foot waterfall, they came to where the West Branch of the Susquehanna merged with the Sinnemahoning. "Take heart, men," the colonel said to his battered crew. "Look at how wide the river gets. We'll have lots more room to maneuver now. Before you know it, we'll be in Lock Haven!"

Chapter Nineteen

GETTING TO HARRISBURG

Three rafts crammed with soldiers floated into Lock Haven and moored at the public dock. As the Bucktails filed onto dry land, they looked more like casualties than the members of a newly formed regiment. Skirmish after skirmish they had fought with the rapids. White water had strafed them. Boulders had bashed them. Waterfalls had blown them sky-high. They had been mercilessly pummeled by an enemy known as the river, and the war had left them drained and hurting.

When Colonel Kane surveyed his limping, spiritless men, he said to Captain Blanchard, "We need to sell the lumber from these rafts and get our regiment some decent food. After we take care of the men, we'll see about procuring rail transportation."

"Yes, sir," agreed the captain. "Where shall we set up camp?"

"Over there is fine," replied the colonel, indicating a grove of trees along the river bank. "Once the men get their fires going, have them get some rest."

After riding down the river with the Cameron County company, Bucky, Jimmy, Curtis, and Boone also bivouacked with them in the shelter of a hemlock thicket. While they crowded around a roaring fire, one of the Cameron men cleared his throat and said, "None of you fellas ever told us how your raft smashed apart like kindlin' wood. We know what you told the colonel, but we figured there was more to it than that."

"It was all that damn Brewer's fault!" said Boone.

"Oh, you mean that fella we buried?"

"Yeah," agreed Jimmy. "He attacked my friend Bucky, here, and knocked our rudder oar apart. I don't know what got into him. Especially after Bucky saved his life."

"He was chock-full of hate," grunted Boone. "He was like a rattler with a broken back, strikin' at anything in reach."

"Yeah, it was Brewer's fault," admitted Curtis. "Neither of us liked you Bucktail brats 'cause we thought you was too young to pull your own weight. We didn't want to go into battle with panicky kids who'd get us killed. But . . . I was wrong about you, Culp. You've got more gumption than a whole gol-dang company of downhomers. After all, us McKean men gotta stick together if we're gonna get through this damn war."

"What did you say about downhomers?" bristled the man from Cameron County.

"Dang!" replied Curtis. "I didn't mean nothin' by it. Don't get yourself all lathered up. Like the colonel said, we gotta save our hate for Johnny Reb."

Curtis held out his hand, and each of the men shook it in turn.

"Say, what's your first name, anyway?" asked Bucky. "All we know you by is 'Sergeant.' "

"Hosea."

"Well, Hosea, we's all glad to finally make your acquaintance."

The men's spirits rose as the warmth from the fires soaked into their bones, and before long their voices joined in boisterous renditions of "Jim Crack Corn" and "Skip to My Lou." Those who didn't sing, pulled their skinning knives from their sheaths and took to whittling or honing their steel blades. Bucky used the time to clean his Kentucky rifle and reminisce about his pa. The evening was perfectly calm, and the men were too content to notice how the setting sun stained the river blood red.

Just before dark, a wagon pulled up to camp, and Colonel Kane jumped down and began yelling for his officers to distribute the food he had fetched from town. There were bags of potatoes, barrels of salt pork, endless loaves of fresh bread, and crocks of homemade jam. As the starved men wolfed down their dinners, they sang their colonel's praises even louder than they had howled out the words to their rowdy songs.

"I wonder where all this food came from?" asked one of the Cameron men at Bucky's fire. "Our regiment ain't got no money to buy nothin'."

"Why, old Colonel Kane is a silver-tongued rascal," said Boone with a wink. "How'd he get the extra lumber for his raft?"

"Yeah," added Jimmy, "I'll bet he could talk Satan out of the password to hell."

"Yep!" grinned Hosea Curtis. "Colonel Kane could charm the bloomers off a schoolmarm. That's for sure!"

Jimmy tried to picture someone sweet-talking stern, old Miss Dempsey from his school in Smethport and cracked up laughing. When the snickering boy fumbled a hunk of steaming pork into the fire, Boone shouted, "Don't worry about it! There's plenty more where that come from!"

"I jess wish there was some liquor to wash it down," sighed Hosea. "I still ain't seen none of that rum ration that Captain Blanchard promised us when we signed the muster roll."

The men gorged themselves until the stars rose and marched halfway across the night sky. When they finally rolled into their blankets, their bellies were full and their faces beaming. Their dreams that night were filled with huge hunks of bread smothered in homemade jam.

The Bucktails woke in the midmorning sun to the bleat of a distant train whistle. The officers had allowed the men to sleep in, and more bread was distributed to them as they re-formed into their proper companies and broke camp. Colonel Kane, riding on Old Glencoe, led them briskly through Lock Haven to the newly constructed train station. A locomotive of the Philadelphia & Erie Railroad puffed impatiently when they marched onto a platform and stood at attention.

Bucky eyed the gaudy gold and maroon engine with trepidation as black smoke belched from a funnel-shaped stack. The hissing hurt his ears, and he wondered at the power inherent in its boiler and driving wheels. Stretched out behind in serpentine fashion were a fuel tender, a string of flatcars loaded with lumber, and three empty boxcars.

"Okay, men," ordered Colonel Kane. "I want you to fall out and board the first two of these boxcars. I rented them to transport you to Harrisburg."

The men compared the smallness of the cars with the large number of them, and a groan rose from the ranks.

"Come on, ladies!" bellowed Captain Blanchard. "You heard the colonel. Get a move on!"

"Damn! How's all of us supposed to fit?" whined a porky Cameron County soldier.

"We'll be packed in like meat in a pot pie," added his husky brother.

"How did we go from four rafts to two little cars?" grumbled another downhomer.

"All right! That's enough!" warned his lieutenant. "Beats walkin', don't it?"

Bucky snuffed at the odor of cattle as he and his companions leaped inside the first of the boxcars. He, Jimmy, and Boone had hustled to enter before the best space was taken. They moved to the right of the sliding door to crouch with their backs against the side of the car. At least they could peek through the slats at the passing countryside and would get a little ventilation.

A hundred and sixty men pushed and shoved and competed for space until every square inch of Bucky's car was occupied with squirming soldiers, unused to such close quarters. It was so crowded, there was no place for the Bucktails to lie down or even stretch out their legs. The engine lurched into gear before the men had a chance to get settled, crashing unseated soldiers down on their neighbors.

The train whistled a forlorn goodbye, pulled out of Lock Haven, and chugged along the West Branch of the Susquehanna River toward Harrisburg. It rocked and swayed until Bucky wanted to throw up. Caged in with all these men, he felt like a beast being taken to slaughter. He turned to peer out the slats of the rolling boxcar, and Jimmy returned his sick smile. Below, the river shimmered in the sun like a coveted jewel, but the chugging engine drowned out the swish of the current and the roar of the powerful rapids.

"How long do you reckon the trip will take?" asked Jimmy after another soldier banged against him when the train lurched around a bend.

"A couple of days, anyhow," said a nearby officer.

"Yeah, if we don't die from the smell of old cattle an' them unwashed downhomers," chuckled Boone.

"Just be glad you're not sittin' in the middle of the car," replied Bucky. "At least we get some fresh air here."

"I'd rather fly over a twenty-foot waterfall any day," said Boone, "than be cooped up in this stinkin' car!"

"That sure was a dandy adventure," agreed Jimmy. "Even though the river was plenty dangerous."

The train bucked again, and the two husky Cameron County soldiers smashed into Hosea Curtis who sat sandwiched between them.

"Damn porkers!" howled Curtis. "Watch where you're rollin'! I seed hogsheads of ale that weighed less than you two!"

"Who are you callin' porkers?" bellowed the heaviest brother.

"Hey, if the fat fits, wear it!"

Enraged, the two brothers began rocking back and forth, squashing Curtis in the middle. Finally, with a squawk, Hosea leaped to his feet and walked over several swearing soldiers to escape the trap.

"Hosea! Over here!" hailed Boone.

"I'm comin'!"

In three bounds Curtis reached the side of the rocking boxcar, precipitating another round of curses. With a growl, the muscular ex-logger intimidated the man beside Boone to move over. Once seated with his own squad, Hosea howled, "Gol-dang train! I'd rather march to Harrisburg than put up with this! It's enough to make a man wish for a good jug of moonshine!"

"Take it easy," snickered Boone, clapping the powerful man on the back, "I thought you'd given up fightin' with the other Bucktails."

"I had until them gol-dang fat boys tried to squish me. Just wait 'til we stop."

"I doubt if we will until we reach Williamsport," replied one of the lieutenants.

"Well, what if I gotta pee before then?" growled Curtis.

"You'll just have to use your hat," kidded Boone.

"What gets me," beefed another soldier, "is that the colonel's horse has a whole boxcar to hisself."

"Well, we don't want him in here with us," said Jimmy.

"Especially when he raises his tail," added Boone with a gap-toothed grin.

Chapter Twenty

TRAINING HAYSEEDS

The train trip to Harrisburg took the better part of two days. The only chance the Bucktails had to stretch their legs was at a brief stopover in Williamsport, and by the time they reached the state capital, they were antsy and spoiling for a fight. When finally they were freed from the boxcars at the Harrisburg station, Bucky, Boone, Curtis, and the others whooped and fired their guns into the air until the officers forced them into rank with the flats of their swords. "Save it for the Rebs," Captain Blanchard bellowed. "Save it for the stinkin' Rebs!"

Colonel Kane marched his men to the tent city known as Camp Curtin that had been growing daily since President Lincoln's call for volunteers in early April. There they endured an endless month of delays while the Army of Pennsylvania decided what to do with them. After they failed to be mustered into service as the 17th Regiment, Colonel Kane became so frustrated that he resigned his commission and entered the army as a private.

"What are we going to do without our leader?" asked Jimmy, after he heard about Kane's resignation. "I don't want to follow anybody else."

"I don't know about you fellas," grunted Curtis, "but I'm sick of this gol-dang stinkin' hole they call Camp Curtin. If the colonel's replacement ain't a straight-shooter, I'm gonna hightail it for home!"

"I'll be right behind you!" shouted Boone.

Because Bucky and his friends were used to the freedom and adventure of the woods, they hated the confinement of Harrisburg with a passion. There were no mountains or woods or deer or elk or raft rides down wild rivers. Even worse, their every movement was dictated by officers who invented an endless series of menial chores for them. After the soldiers had endured a particularly difficult day, Hosea Curtis stomped back to the McKean Company bivouac and growled, "If I gotta jump to one more gol-dang order, I'm gonna wring that little rooster of a lieutenant's neck!"

"Why, what did he make you do today?" asked Jimmy.

"I stood guard over a tentful of gol-dang spoiled beef!"

"That can't be any worse than diggin' rocks from the parade ground," said Bucky.

"Or polishing fifty officers' boots," added Jimmy.

"It's almost like we's prisoners," griped Hosea. "Where's all the liberty that the colonel promised us? I ain't had a stiff drink in a month of Sundays!"

"I wish we were at least allowed out of camp to kill some fresh meat," said Bucky.

"Yeah, army rations just don't stand up to venison," agreed Boone.

The men equally hated the instruction they received in close formation drilling. Whole afternoons were spent saluting sergeants, standing at attention, marching to the left, marching to the right, advancing as a group, or retreating as a group. These maneuvers seldom went smoothly because many of the woodsmen didn't know one foot from the other. Finally, after the ranks ended up in a horrendous snarl, a frustrated drill instructor barked, "You Bucktails are the most pitiful group of recruits I ever seed! You got about as much discipline as bucks in the rut! Looks like the only way you're gonna march in cadence is if we makes a game of it."

"A game?" grumbled Hosea Curtis. "I thought we came here to kill Rebs, not play 'Ring Around the Rosie.'"

The officer told Curtis to shut his "pie hole" and ordered the soldiers to tie hay on their left boots and straw on their right boots. "Okay!" he bellowed. "Now I want you to repeat after me:

> March! March! March!
> Old soldiers march!
> Hayfoot, strawfoot,
> Belly full of bean soup—
> March, old soldier, march!"

"This is like being back in nursery school," giggled Jimmy.

"If we do this in a battle, we won't even have to fire a shot," chuckled Boone. "The Rebels'll laugh themselves to death."

"Silence!" barked the drill instructor. "All you idiots gotta do is repeat the words and move your feet to 'em. Just pretend you're at a barn dance. That is if there are barns where you boys come from."

The officer led the Bucktails around the parade ground for two more hours until their throats were raw from shouting "March! March! March!" When they finally moved in sync, he ordered them to stay in formation and file to another practice field. There they learned how to fix a bayonet on the end of a rifle and how to plunge it into the chest of a straw dummy. "That drill should come in real handy if we ever has to fight a scarecrow," observed Boone wryly.

When Bucky and his friends were squatting in front of their tents that evening, they saw a large company of men dressed in buckskin straggle into camp. "Hey, where are you fellas from?" asked Boone of one of the passing woodsmen.

"We's from Warren up on the Allegheny. We's come with Captain Stone to fight Johnny Reb."

"Why, that's further than we come!"

"Yep! We floated downriver on flatboats to Pittsburgh and then marched across the whole dang state of Pennsylvany."

"Well, I'll be dipped in sour owl manure," whistled Curtis. "Maybe we'll see you boys around. I got a feelin' we's all gonna be here for awhile."

The weeks passed, and Camp Curtin continued to swell in size as more and more recruits poured in from all parts of the state. Thomas Kane asked the governor to restore his commission and resumed command of the McKean, Elk, and Cameron soldiers. When the company captains from Warren, Chester, Perry, Clearfield, Carbon, and Tioga Counties grew weary of the same delays that had faced Kane's men, they proposed that they band together and form a skirmish outfit. To this purpose, they submitted a letter to General McCall:

> The undersigned, captains of companies now in Camp Curtin, present their respects to Major General M'Call, congratulating the army of Pennsylvania upon being placed under such a commander. They beg not to be supposed desirous of interfering with Major General M'Call's discretion in expressing a desire to have their companies united to form one regiment under the command of Colonel Thomas L. Kane. They are assured that their men are peculiarly qualified to serve efficiently in a regiment of rifles under Colonel Kane, being, with few exceptions, men of extremely hardy habits and trained from boyhood to the use of arms.

The next day, the McKean County Company was summoned by Captain Blanchard to participate in a general election of officers for the newly formed Bucktail Regiment. After they had voted, Bucky, Jimmy, Hosea Curtis, and Boone paced nervously back and forth waiting for the results to be announced.

"Do you think Kane will be chosen as our colonel?" asked Jimmy as he fussed with a loose button on his shirt.

"Hell, yeah!" reassured Boone. "He's a shoe-in!"

"But do you think he'll accept?" asked Hosea. "Rumor has it that he'd soonest have Biddle take over."

"Why Biddle?" asked Jimmy.

"'Cause he's got battle experience in the war with them Mexicans. I think that if Kane is elected colonel, he'll resign in favor of that old war horse, Biddle."

Curtis was right because the next day the men were summoned to yet another election. Thomas Kane indeed had resigned his commission, and before the men revoted, he visited the camp of each company to enlist support for the man he thought most qualified to lead the Bucktails.

This act of generosity did not go unrewarded. After Biddle was elected colonel and Thomas Kane lieutenant colonel, the captains of the various companies petitioned the War Department that their regimental name be officially changed from the First Rifles to the Kane Rifle Regiment of the Pennsylvania Reserve Corps. Bucky, Curtis, and many of the McKean men fired a volley into the air when this petition was read aloud by Captain Blanchard. The men cheered and howled for Lieutenant Colonel Kane to acknowledge this honor in person.

"Men," boomed Kane, "I believe officers should be long on action and short on speeches. This is a great honor bestowed on us . . . yes, us. In no small measure, this is your honor. It binds us into one fighting unit. This unit will know no equal in valor, honor, or dedication. Men, I say without fear of contradiction, that the Kane Rifle Regiment is bound for glory fighting the good fight for freedom. May God bless our regiment."

After the Bucktails were officially sworn into the Army of Pennsylvania, they were taken to a depot and issued their uniforms. Each man was given a white flannel shirt, a dark blue coat, light blue button-fly trousers, a riflemen's pouch, a knapsack, a canteen, a set of suspenders, and a hat which they promptly decorated with deer hide.

"Hey, look at the gol-dang tiny coat they give me!" bellowed Hosea Curtis after the men received their clothing. "I can't even git it over one shoulder."

"And mine is the size of a tent!" squawked Boone.

"Come on, Crossmire, be a good fella and swap with me," wheedled Curtis. "Ah! That's better. Fits perfect."

"Look what Jimmy's got," said Bucky as his friend stepped toward them rat-tat-tating his very own army regulation snare drum.

"And they even gave me my own drummer's sword," beamed Jimmy.

"Just make sure you don't lose it like you did your Smith & Wesson pistol," teased Bucky.

"Aw, I'm not interested in drinking anymore."

"In that case, make sure I gets your rum ration if'n they ever give us one!" exclaimed Hosea.

When the soldiers turned to leave the depot, they were accosted by a belligerent officer who barked, "Hold it right there. You men have forgotten to turn in your weapons."

"What'd ya mean turn 'em in?" snarled Hosea. "What'd ya want us to do? Blow kisses at them Rebels?"

"Those rifles aren't government issue," snapped the officer. "They'll have to be sent home."

"I can't give up my Kentucky beauty," blustered Boone. "She's the only one's been faithful to me in my whole life."

"Yeah!" yelled Frank. "You might as well take my right arm while you're at it."

Bucky swallowed hard when his turn came to give up his gun. He had always been totally confident in its accuracy, and it had served as a lasting reminder of his pa. He had won his way into the army with it, too, and had used it to feed himself and his comrades in arms. No target within two hundred yards was safe from its lethal kiss. It was his friend and protector and responded to his touch like a living thing. The depot workers had to practically pry the rifle out of Bucky's fingers after he had told them he wanted it sent to the Jewetts for safekeeping.

The grumbling McKean men were given fifty-eight caliber Springfield and Enfield muskets to replace their personal guns. "Your new weapons are far superior to those we collected from you," assured the issuing officer. "They fire a Minie ball that is much easier to reload than the bullet used in the Kentucky rifle. The Minie ball comes wrapped in a paper cartridge that contains the charge of gunpowder. This will eliminate the need for measuring out powder from a clumsy horn while you're fighting in a battle. Such rapid reloading just might save your lives."

"But how do we know these gol-dang muskets can shoot straight?" asked Hosea.

"Yeah!" griped Boone. "If they ain't accurate, all that rapid reloadin' ain't gonna do us no good."

As the men stormed through the tent village back to their bivouac lugging their new muskets, an excited courier rushed up to them and asked directions to Colonel Biddle's quarters. "What's goin' on?" asked Curtis. "You can tell us."

"It ain't gonna be a big secret, anyhow!" exclaimed the courier. "J.E.B. Stuart just rode clean around the Union army. He's burnin' supplies. Cuttin' communications. McClellan is fit to be tied!"

"Won't be long now, boys," said Hosea knowingly. "Sharpshooters like us is gonna be in real demand before you can say gol-dang Jefferson Davis."

Chapter Twenty-One
PLUNGED INTO BATTLE

Bucky and Jimmy backed the Federal wagon into a dilapidated barn. They jumped to the ground and then climbed ten rickety steps to a loft crammed with hay. When the soldiers began pitching the hay down to Frank and Boone, who waited below to load it into the wagon, an enraged female screamed from the yard, "What gives you the right?"

"Ma'am, by order of the government of these United States, we do requisition your hay," came the curt but polite reply of Lieutenant Ward.

"If you-all's that hungry that you have to eat hay, step into the kitchen, and I'll fix you blue bellies some nice grits."

"The hay is for the mounts of the U.S. Cavalry," said the lieutenant, reddening.

"And what's my poor cattle supposed to eat all winter?"

"Take it up with headquarters, ma'am. I'm only following orders."

"Just like every other damn Yankee that's overrunning Dranesville! Wait 'til our boys catch up with you! You won't have any cavalry left to ride them mounts!"

Pricked by the woman's angry voice, Bucky and Jimmy hustled about their task until half the hay had been tossed to their fellow soldiers. "We got room for a little more," shouted the lieutenant up the steps.

"Sorry," replied Bucky. "There ain't no more."

"But our scouts said—"

"The scouts exaggerated," said Jimmy, with a wink at his friend.

Bucky and Jimmy climbed down to the ground, brushing the chaff from their uniforms. As they rejoined their squad, Bucky said, "I hate this forage detail. It makes me feel like a chicken thief."

"Yeah," agreed Boone. "I thought we joined the army to fight Rebs, not steal from poor folk."

"It's not Christian," said Jimmy.

"All right, quit your jabbering!" interrupted Lieutenant Ward. "Fall back in line! We got a lot more farms to visit before we get our five wagons loaded."

Bucky shivered in the damp December wind, although he felt a lot more at home here in northern Virginia than he had in Harrisburg. Here there were rolling hills and lots of woods. Small game was plentiful, too, and he had snared enough of it to return to his usual meat diet.

While the Bucktails moved off down the road, Bucky could still hear the angry farmer's wife cursing Yankees. He smiled when he thought of how surprised she would be when she found half of her hay stored in its usual place.

"Where're we off to now, Lieutenant?" Bucky asked, seeing that they had veered off onto the Leesburg pike.

"We're going to rejoin the main column and have lunch. This deep in Reb territory, General Ord didn't want us straying too far."

Lieutenant Ward's command consisted of five wagons and three squads of Bucktailed riflemen. When they rattled around the next bend, they could see other similar units gathering in an oak grove just off the road. Less than a quarter of a mile in the distance, the town of Dranesville was visible through the bare limbs of the trees. A stone fence bordered the road, and a small pasture lay to the right.

When given permission to leave their ranks, Jimmy and Bucky joined Curtis and his squad around a roaring fire. The men joked and exchanged accounts of their morning. From this vantage point, they could see General Ord and Lieutenant Colonel Kane discussing strategies beneath a makeshift canvas lean-to. Stretched out before the officers on a stump was a map that Ord poked at vigorously with his index finger. His deep-set eyes glowed intensely beneath a furrowed brow as he made a sweeping gesture, and then he pointed at the field artillery hooked to their caissons.

The officers' discussion was interrupted by peals of thunder in the adjacent wood when a concealed Confederate battery burst into life. Cannon balls screamed into the Union camp like errant meteors, throwing up fountains of earth and scattering Ord's troops. With his gray mustache bristling, the general screamed out orders and waved his arms like a windmill caught in a gale. Before the second Rebel barrage ripped the wood, his own artillery was brought to bear on the enemy position.

Lieutenant Colonel Kane, meanwhile, screeched to his Bucktails, "Hurry, men! To the right flank! This way!"

Bucky and Jimmy ran low to the ground until they found suitable places of concealment, while their officers barked orders and the Union cannons spewed smoke and bright fire. The Confederate battery continued to growl and grumble and rain lethal projectiles down on the Yankees. It was lucky for Bucky and his buddies that they scrambled when they did, for the fire where they swapped stories just moments before disintegrated in a direct hit from a Confederate field piece.

The Rebel and Union artillery traded barrages for the next half-hour. Cannon balls splintered trees, threw up earth, and scared the devil out of the troops. Bucky hunkered behind a sturdy oak to weather the storm. He could see Jimmy, with his fingers stuffed in his ears, lying behind a low stone wall.

Bucky flinched at a particularly close shot and turned to watch a cannon ball bounce past him across the battlefield. He shuddered when he thought of the green soldier he had heard about in Harrisburg who had stuck out his foot to stop a rolling round shot, only to lose his leg in the process.

Luckily, the Confederates concentrated most of their fire on the Union artillery position. Bucky could see the gun crews sweating in the pale sunlight as they reloaded and fired their twelve-pound Napoleon field howitzers three to four times a minute while ducking the plumes of earth that rose from around their guns. One Yankee cannon lay out of commission on its side. It had been demolished in the first five minutes of combat. Its crew looked like broken puppets, lying bleeding where they'd been blown. One poor gunner lay over the smashed fieldpiece with only a stump where his head had been moments before.

When the bombardment stopped, Bucky's ears felt like they were stuffed with cotton. He had trouble hearing the thud of his own heartbeat. It was equally difficult to see with the powder smoke that hung like fog on the battlefield. The Rebs used this poor visibility to their advantage, and Bucky could just make out the orange muzzle flashes of Confederate skirmishers who slunk forward through the woods like gray-coated wolves. Although an excellent snap shot, Bucky failed to draw a bead on the illusive Reb soldiers who dodged stealthily from tree to tree. Minie balls whined through the undergrowth and ricocheted off rocks until fear churned like venom in Bucky's guts.

Jimmy lay behind the low stone wall cradling his drum. Although receiving his baptism of fire months before, he still had not grown accustomed to the noise and smoke of battle. White-faced, Jimmy trembled in his soiled blue jacket until Hosea Curtis mocked from behind an uprooted stump, "What's wrong? Mama's boy scared?"

Jimmy winced as a bullet caromed off the top of the stone wall. He was sweating like a dysentery patient, and fear glittered in his wide brown eyes. He looked ready to run when he glanced pleadingly at Bucky for support.

Bucky lunged from his refuge and rolled recklessly to his beleaguered friend, igniting another volley of Rebel fire. Again, the angry whine of bullets cut the air, and Hosea filled the afternoon with epithets when a ball creased his scalp and another took off the toe of his boot. A man of six-foot-five should have known better than to have chosen such a little stump for cover. But instead of blaming himself, he howled, "Gol-dang you, Jimmy! Why couldn't you have stayed home with mama!"

Bucky lay face down next to Jimmy, listening to the crack of rifles and the groan of the wounded. He shivered from his close escape and motioned for Curtis to join them behind the wall. Hosea crouched like a puma, then sprung next to Bucky with the surprising agility often produced by fear. He was still cussing Jimmy when safely concealed from Rebel fire.

"Why are you blaming me?" whined Jimmy. "We Bucktails are always in the thick of it, getting stuck with the dirty jobs."

"What did you expect when you joined?" snarled Curtis. "A Sunday social?"

"N-o-o-o!"

"Well, Colonel Kane told us from the beginning that we'd be used as scouts, skirmishers, and shock troops."

"Yeah," added Bucky. "That was our job when we routed McDonald's cavalry at New Creek Village and drove the Lousy-ana Zouaves from Hunter's Mill."

"Yeah, we's regular wildcats, we is," boasted Hosea. "An' old J.E.B. Stuart's boys better watch out here, too, or we'll give them a shellacking they won't soon forget."

The Rebels renewed their howling, and Bucky peered over the wall to see them charging forward in a ragged gray line. Bucky fired at a Reb leaping a fallen log. He kept his head exposed just long enough to watch the soldier throw up his arms and crumble into a heap. Then he began feverishly reloading his musket, keeping his arm well below the wall while he worked the ramrod.

A grin gleamed on Bucky's powder-begrimed face when Curtis took a quick shot and bellowed, "Got him! Got that gol-dang Reb peckerwood! These Enfields sure is sweet-shootin' guns, even though they took some gettin' used to."

"Yeah," agreed Bucky. "Don't you remember how some of the fellas blew that cavalry officer out of the saddle at a thousand yards with their Enfields?"

"You bet I do!" guffawed Curtis. "That was back in October. Though a dozen men fired that volley, naturally old Boone took credit for killin' the 5th Virginny Cap'in."

Bucky and Curtis continued to lay down a withering fire until Lieutenant Colonel Kane rushed up to their position and began motioning with his sword toward a brick house off to their right. "Hurry up!" he barked. "That house is only a hundred yards from our lines! The Rebs can't be allowed to capture it, or we're finished!"

Lieutenant Colonel Kane moved like a man possessed as he gathered twenty men and rushed forward to occupy the house. He exposed himself unnecessarily, charging straight across open ground to reach his objective. Curtis was right at his leader's heels, screaming like he'd gone berserk. Bucky and Jimmy followed in a more indirect route, keeping to the cover until they reached the rest of the unit lying in the shadows of the brick mansion.

The Bucktails hugged the ground when three regiments of Confederate infantry rushed through the woods toward them. The Rebs screeched like banshees during their advance, waving banners and brandishing their swords and muskets. The officers wore plumes in their felt hats and screamed even louder than their battle-crazed men.

When the Rebels closed within two hundred yards, the Bucktails fired a volley that caved in the center of the onrushing ranks. Ten riflemen fell like a row of scythed wheat. A flagman spun like a weather vane and fell on his face. A burly captain was blown backward by three balls to the chest. A lieutenant took another shot through the throat. His Rebel yell was replaced by a gurgling wheeze. He collapsed and was trampled by the men behind him.

Within three minutes, three volleys left the Rebels reeling and in disarray. Hosea Curtis picked off three Confederate officers with three shots, while Bucky knocked down three Rebel flag bearers. Both men fired and reloaded with machinelike precision. The enemy soldiers were simply targets that had to be stopped. They felt no compassion for those clothed in the gray coats of wolves.

When the Rebels began to fall back, Lieutenant Colonel Kane leaped to his feet and shouted, "We got 'em on the run, men! Charge! Charge!"

The words were no sooner bellowed than a Rebel ball smashed through Kane's face and down through the roof of his mouth. The same volley knocked half a dozen Bucktails groaning to the earth. The Minie balls were so thick around them they sounded like a swarm of disturbed hornets. Jimmy's drum was splintered by four balls, while Bucky's hat was blown from his head. "Now you done it!" howled Hosea when a bullet grazed his cheek and another glanced off his gun stock. "You're gonna pay, you gol-dang Rebs!"

Kane stumbled only for a moment. Yanking a handkerchief from his pocket, he stanched the flow of blood, raised his sword, and leaped forward with his men roaring at his heels. The Rebels were now in panicked retreat, barely saving a field cannon from capture as the Bucktails swept down on them. Their dead and wounded littered the ground behind them when they fled.

Drunk with combat, Bucky raced too far ahead of his regiment and suddenly found himself surrounded by the Rebs' rear guard. They came howling at him from all sides, jabbing with their bayonets. Bucky blew half a soldier's head off at point blank range and beat two others to the ground with the butt of his rifle. While he fended off an officer with a saber, a fourth Rebel drove his bayonet through Bucky's oversized blue tunic, barely missing his ribs. "Take that, you damn Yankee!" grunted the Confederate infantryman.

Jimmy had lagged behind the charging Bucktails, holding his smashed drum in front of him like a shield. When he saw Bucky was about to be swarmed under, he slammed his drum to the ground and scooped up a discarded Confederate musket. With a screech he leaped forward, swinging his weapon like a club. His adrenalin made him stronger than men twice his size, and he bashed in two troopers' skulls before they could turn to defend themselves.

Bucky had been knocked to the ground, and two more Rebels came at him with their bayonets poised for the kill. He rolled at the last instant to avoid his assailants, just as Hosea Curtis leaped from the powder smoke to blast both Rebs with one shot.

Bucky, Jimmy, and Hosea formed a defensive circle, only to watch the remaining Confederates melt away into the woods. "Gol-dang Rebs has had enough!" shouted Hosea. "We done it, boys!"

"Indeed you have, *Sergeant* Curtis," gurgled Lieutenant Colonel Kane, emerging from the gunpowder fog. "You may resume command of your squad. I need wildcats like you to lead my men."

"Thank you, sir!"

After spitting a gob of bright blood, Kane turned to Jimmy and choked, "Well, done, Jewett. I expect you've traded in your drum permanently?"

"Yes, sir!"

"Forward, Culp. Let's see if we can drive these Rebels back to hell!"

Chapter Twenty-Two
Where's Jimmy?

The Bucktails continued to chase the Rebels four miles out of Dranesville until Lieutenant Colonel Kane collapsed in mid-stride. "Hold up, men!" screamed Captain Blanchard, stooping to aid his superior officer. "Curtis! Culp! Get over here! Give the colonel a hand!"

Bucky and Hosea hoisted Colonel Kane to his feet and helped him limp back toward the Union lines. The ground behind them was littered with Rebel dead and wounded that the Confederates abandoned in their chaotic retreat. The colonel, though, was well beyond noticing them. Blood dribbled from the corner of his mouth, and his usually fiery eyes were dull and listless.

The soldiers assisted their leader to a field hospital set up behind the artillery position. A pile of amputated arms and legs lay outside the surgeons' tent, and the smell of blood and decaying flesh made Bucky nauseous. Inside the tent, a man screamed as if his soul were in mortal danger. Finally, a doctor howled, "Hold him down! Knock that man out with some ether!"

Two orderlies emerged from one of the hospital tents and helped Lieutenant Colonel Kane onto a bloody cot. "Take care of yourself, sir," said Sergeant Curtis before he and Bucky turned to go back to the regiment. Kane nodded vaguely and slipped into unconsciousness.

147

As Bucky and Hosea stumbled through the hospital compound, Hosea said, "All that fightin' sure made me powerful thirsty."

"I still have a little water left in my canteen," offered Bucky. "Want some?"

"No! I need somethin' a lot stronger than water to wash the powder smoke from this here throat! Hell! The main reason I joined the army was 'cause Cap'in Blanchard promised we'd have what he called a *liberal rum ration*. He must have been talkin' through his hat, 'cause I ain't seen even one drop of it yet."

"Well, if you ever get yourself wounded, you can have all the whiskey you want. It's rumored them surgeons get their patients roarin' drunk before they break out their meat saws."

"No, thanks," cringed Hosea. "Maybe I'll become a teetotaler yet."

Bucky and Hosea hurried past several hospital tents before entering the shattered grove where the battle had begun. There they overheard an off-duty surgeon remark to an artillery captain, "Our boys must have given them Confederates a whippin'. We've treated twice as many of their wounded."

"Yeah," replied the captain. "General Ord said that we only lost seven men, while we killed over forty Rebs."

"I guess them Bucktails really saved our bacon today when the Rebs tried to flank us."

"The general himself said they're the best sharpshooters this side of hell."

Bucky and Hosea grinned at each other and hightailed it back to the battlefield to look for Jimmy and the rest of their squad. A few men they recognized limped past them toward the hospital, but as far as they knew, all their closest friends had escaped the battle unscathed.

Darkness was closing in on them fast when Bucky and Hosea found Boone and several others from their company gathered around a roaring fire. "Have you boys seed Jimmy?" asked Frank and handed the newcomers cups of diluted coffee.

"No, I thought he was here with you," said Bucky with alarm. "I'd better try to find him."

Frank and Boone snatched up their rifles and said, "Hey, wait for us!"

Bucky, Hosea, Frank, and Boone spread out into a skirmish line and began working their way across the battlefield, pausing often to examine the still unburied dead. They had gone maybe five hundred yards in the direction the Rebels had retreated when they saw three shadows step from a misty patch of woods.

"Who goes there?" shouted Hosea, drawing back the hammer on his rifle.

"Don't shoot!" echoed a familiar voice from the fog. "It's me . . . Jimmy!"

"Who's with you?" asked Bucky.

"Prisoners!"

"Well, I'll be gol-danged!" exclaimed Hosea. "The little fella done caught hisself a coupla Rebs."

Jimmy marched forward prodding two Confederate officers in the back with his cocked rifle. "Caught these men skulking around in the brush over there. They won't tell me who they are, but the tall one here has captain's bars on his shoulders."

"By gum, you're right," grinned Boone. "If that don't beat all!"

"Headquarters is over yonder," said Frank, gesturing behind him. "Do you want help with your prisoners?"

"No, I'm fine."

"You heard the man!" shouted Hosea. "He can de-liver them hisself!"

"Get movin'," commanded Jimmy. "We haven't got far to go now."

As Jimmy herded the Rebs toward headquarters, the others returned to their campfire to swill coffee, reminisce about the battle, and discuss the future.

"A tough day!" exclaimed Frank, plopping on the ground next to the fire.

"How many from our regiment did we lose?" asked Hosea. "We heard at the hospital that the Rebs lost six times more men than we did."

"Company B lost Galbraith and Raup. Twenty-some others was wounded," replied Boone.

"How's Colonel Kane?" asked Frank with a concerned frown.

"Not good," replied Bucky.

"What'll we do if he . . . don't make it?" wondered Boone.

"Don't worry about that," said Hosea. "He's a tough nut. How many other men would have kept chargin' after gettin' shot square in the face?"

"Yeah, the colonel'll be back, all right," agreed Frank.

"But what'll happen to us in the meantime?" asked Bucky.

"Oh, we'll probably get shipped back to Harrisburg, is my guess," replied Hosea.

"To do what?" groaned Bucky.

"I heard tell Colonel Kane is working on some new skirmish tactics," said Frank. "He'll probably have us learn them while he's laid up."

"Where did you hear that?" scoffed Hosea.

"Right from the horse's mouth."

"I didn't know Old Glencoe could talk," chortled Boone.

"No! No! I overheard the colonel tellin' Captain Blanchard about 'em."

"With big ears like that," kidded Boone, "you oughta be a spy."

"But they shoot spies, don't they?" asked Bucky. "Frank would never go for that."

"Oh, why don't you fellas go suck an egg!"

"Wherever we end up, boys," added Hosea in a grave voice, "we gotta stick together."

"Why's that?" asked Boone.

"'Cause we got the best gol-dang regiment in this here Union army! Just ask General Ord!"

"You better believe it," agreed Boone. "Why, even Jimmy turned out to be a gen-uine hero."

"Speakin' of Jimmy," said Bucky, rising to his feet, "maybe I'd better see what become of him. It shouldn't have taken him this long to deliver them prisoners."

"Yeah, I think you should go," said Boone with a mischievous wink. "He's probably gonna need some help to get back here."

"How come?"

"When Jimmy took them captured Rebs up to head-quarters, I'll bet General Ord pinned so many medals on his chest he ain't able to move!"

With a chuckle Bucky wandered across the Union camp toward a group of lantern-lit tents near the hospital compound. He ambled along and surveyed each group of faces gathered around the many campfires he passed. The soldiers joked and bragged and filled the night with jubilation. Although Jimmy had earned the right to celebrate with the rest of the regiment, he was nowhere to be found among the victory-intoxicated Bucktails.

Finally, Bucky spotted his missing friend sitting behind a makeshift table outside the officers' tent. He was poring over a piece of brown wrapping paper he had in front of him:

Dear Mother,

Please excuse the paper I'm using, but things are in short supply right now. I write from a small place in Virginia called Dranesville. It's nothing to see and surely isn't a place to die for. We fought the Rebs here and sent them running. Bucky and I got through the battle. We didn't

run. We fought like men. Bucky is a true friend
and my protector. I try to be the same for him.

I was able to capture two Rebels myself. It
wasn't such a great feat, but the other men seem
to think I'm a hero. I know Father would tell me
pride is a sinful thing, but I'm not bragging. I'm
just telling you what happened.

Mother, war isn't the great adventure I
thought it was going to be. I've seen suffering I
never believed was possible. Now I know that is
why you were trying to protect me. You weren't
trying to stop me from growing up but wanted to
spare me this pain. Please forgive me for not
understanding.

There is one other thing. Will you and Father
pray for Colonel Kane? He was shot in the battle.
He's the great man I thought he was. We never
would have won today without his courage. All of
us Bucktails will miss him while he's recovering
from his wounds.

I'll write again soon.

                                        Jimmy

Jimmy never looked up until Bucky said, "What are ya
readin'?"

"A letter to my mother. I figured I'd tell her about the
battle now that I'm a real soldier instead of a drummer boy."

"I'll bet she'll be mighty proud."

"I don't know about that, but at least maybe she won't
worry so much about me now that I've proved I can take
care of myself."

"Did you tell her how you helped save my skin? I never
did get a chance to thank ya."

"Yeah, I did mention that . . . a little."

"What did Captain Blanchard say when you brought in
them Rebs?"

"Not much. He was too concerned about Colonel Kane to pay much attention to me. He did seem surprised, though."

"Well, I wasn't, Jimmy. I knew you had a lot of grit when you left home like you did. I never could figure out why you give up your life in Smethport . . . until today."

"I just wish I was there when all those rough boys at school hear how we clobbered the Rebels."

"I don't think you have to worry about bullies no more. When you get home, they'll be the ones who's in awe of you. Where do you think we'll be headin' now that Colonel Kane is laid up?"

"Probably back to Harrisburg."

"That's what Hosea said. That sure don't make me very happy. I had about all of them 'Hayfoot, Strawfoot' drills I can stand."

"Yeah," snickered Jimmy. "Me too. But I don't think they ask heroes like us Bucktails to do much drilling."

"Now you're startin' to sound like Boone," teased Bucky. "If you're done writin', let's get back before our buddies swill all the coffee."

"Okay. Just let me duck inside this tent and give my letter to one of the officers. You know, Bucky, in a way we found ourselves a family here, too, even though I'd never admit that to Hosea, Frank, or Boone."

"I reckon they feel the same way," said Bucky. "Wherever my pa is, I know he's glad I'm fightin' alongside such a good bunch of fellas."

Bibliography

Angle, Paul M. *A Pictorial History of the Civil War Years*. Garden City, N.Y.: Doubleday & Company, Inc., 1967.

Arnett, Hazel. *I Hear American Singing*. New York: Praeger Publishing, Inc., 1975.

Athearn, Robert G. *The Civil War*. New York: Choice Publishing, Inc., 1988.

Bates, Samuel P. *History of Pennsylvania Volunteers 1861– 1865*. 5 vols. Harrisburg, Pa.: B. Singerly, State Printer, 1869.

Billings, John D. *Hard Tack and Coffee*. Boston: George M. Smith & Co., 1887.

Botkin, B. A., ed. *A Civil War Treasury of Tales, Legends and Folklore*. New York: Random House, 1960.

Bowman, John S., ed. *The Civil War Day by Day*. Greenwich, Conn.: Dorset Press, 1989.

Brandt, Dennis W. "The Bucktail Regiment." *Potter County Historical Society Quarterly Bulletin*, January 1998, pp. 2–3.

Burgess, George H., and Miles C. Kennedy. *Centennial History of the Pennsylvania Railroad Company 1846– 1946*. Philadelphia: The Pennsylvania Railroad Company, 1949.

155

Catton, Bruce. *The Army of the Potomac: Mr. Lincoln's Army.* Garden City, N.Y.: Doubleday & Company, Inc., 1962.

Chamberlin, Lieutenant Colonel Thomas. *History of the One Hundred and Fiftieth Regiment Pennsylvania Volunteers, Second Regiment, Bucktail Brigade.* Philadelphia: F. McManus, Jr. & Company, 1905.

Commager, Henry Steele. *The Blue and the Gray.* 2 vols. New York: The Fairfax Press, 1982.

Glover, Edwin A. *Bucktailed Wildcats: A Regiment of Civil War Volunteers.* New York: Thomas Yoseloff, 1960.

History of the Counties of McKean, Elk, Cameron and Potter, Pennsylvania. 2 vols. Chicago: J. H. Beers & Co. Publishers, 1890.

Leish, Kenneth W., ed. *The American Heritage Songbook.* New York: American Heritage Publishing Company, Inc., 1969.

Lord, Francis A. *Civil War Collector's Encyclopedia.* New York: Castle Books, 1965.

McClellan, Elisabeth. *History of American Costume 1607–1870.* New York: Tudor Publishing Company, 1937.

Menge, W. Springer, and J. August Shimrak, eds. *The Civil War Notebook of Daniel Chrisholm.* New York: Orion Books, 1989.

Nofi, Albert A. *The Civil War Treasury.* New York: Mallard Press, 1990.

O'Shea, Richard. *Battle Maps of the Civil War.* Tulsa: Council Oak Books, 1992.

Stone, Rufus Barrett. *McKean: The Governor's County.* New York: Lewis Historical Publishing Company, Inc., 1926.

Thomson, O. R. Howard, and William H. Rauch. *History of the Bucktails.* Philadelphia: Electric Printing Company, 1906.

The Union Army. 8 vols. Madison, Wisc.: Federal Publishing Company, 1908.

Van Doren Stern, Phillip, ed. *Soldier Life in the Union and Confederate Armies.* Bloomington: Indiana University Press, 1961.

Warner, Ezra J. *Generals in Blue.* Baton Rouge: Louisiana State University Press, 1964.

Wilcox, R. Turner. *Five Centuries of American Costume.* New York: Charles Scribner's Sons, 1963.

The Authors

An award-winning author of both poetry and prose published in seven countries, **William P. Robertson** is also widely experienced in communicating American heritage to children. He is a graduate of Mansfield University and has taught in the Otto-Eldred and Bradford School Districts in Pennsylvania. He has been a student of the Civil War since childhood and is currently a self-employed housepainter.

An experienced teacher, author, and editor, **David Rimer** is a graduate of Clarion and Edinboro Universities in Pennsylvania. He has also been a lifelong student of the Civil War.

Also by the Authors

Jimmy and Bucky's Adventures Continue:

The Bucktails' Shenandoah March
(978-1-57249-293-6, PB)

After enduring the boredom of winter camp, Bucky Culp and Jimmy Jewett's company of Pennsylvania Bucktails under Lieutenant Colonel Thomas Kane trek to the Shenandoah Valley in pursuit of the legendary General Thomas J. "Stonewall" Jackson. Using Kane's new technique of being "foot cavalry," Bucky and Jimmy are thoroughly tested by the privations of forced marches, the loss of a beloved comrade, the imprisonment of their lieutenant colonel, and bitter defeats that decimated the ranks of the proud Bucktails.

The Bucktails' Antietam Trials
(978-1-57249-337-7; PB)

Corporal Bucky Culp wasn't exaggerating when he called the deserter Whalen "the worst sort of varmint." Whalen's cowardice caused Bucky's best friend to be wounded at Antietam, and now the rascal brought shame on the whole regiment by attacking the farm girl Sarah Pfaff. Little did Bucky realize when he rescued Sarah that soon she would fill a major void in his life.

The Battling Bucktails at Fredericksburg
(978-1-57249-345-2; PB)

This fourth novel of the Pennsylvania Bucktail series focuses on the courage and tenacity of the volunteer soldiers who suffered from every conceivable deprivation and yet persevered. Bucky Culp overcomes his emotional anguish, Jimmy Jewett survives severe spiritual doubts, and Boone Crossmire endures the loss of his best friend to live up to their reputation as "the battling Bucktails."

CPSIA information can be obtained
at www.ICGtesting.com
Printed in the USA
BVHW04s2339060418
512747BV00003B/3/P

9 781572 492509